Bad Moon Rising

Piper saw a thick, enormous black snake rear up beside the flickering fire.

"What kind of snake is that?" Piper asked.

"It . . . it looks like the creature from my vision," Phoebe told her. "The snake that was going to devour that girl."

"That's no snake. It's a *loa*, an evil voodoo spirit," Randy muttered. The monstrous creature turned its head toward them. Its eyes were twin pinpoints of flame. Deadly fangs jutted from its mouth. Piper had never seen anything that was so purely evil.

"It's seen us!" Yvonne exclaimed. "This is it. You must use your power now if we are to escape."

Stepping out of the shadows, the three Halliwell sisters joined hands. They advanced slowly on the loa.

"The Power of Three," Piper called out to steel her sisters. They squeezed her hands.

"The Power of Three," they answered back.

Charmed™

The Power of Three
A novelization by Eliza Willard

Kiss of Darkness
By Brandon Alexander

The Crimson Spell
By F. Goldsborough

Whispers from the Past
By Rosalind Noonan

Voodoo Moon
By Wendy Corsi Staub

Pocket Pulse
Published by Pocket Books

VOODOO MOON

An original novel by Wendy Corsi Staub
Based on the hit TV series
created by Constance M. Burge

A Parachute Press Book

POCKET PULSE
New York London Toronto Sydney Singapore

An *Original* Publication of POCKET BOOKS

 POCKET PULSE published by
Pocket Books, a division of Simon & Schuster Inc.
1230 Avenue of the Americas, New York, NY 10020

™ & © 2000 Spelling Television Inc. All Rights Reserved.

ISBN: 0-671-04166-5

First Pocket Pulse printing August 2000

10 9 8 7 6 5 4 3 2 1

POCKET PULSE and colophon are trademarks of
Simon & Schuster Inc.

Printed in the U.S.A.

VOODOO MOON

CHAPTER
1

Prue Halliwell rolled down her window, stuck out her head, and glared at the driver of the sleek black sports car behind her. The driver was leaning on his horn—again—as he had been on and off for the last ten minutes.

Great. Keep honking, buddy—because that will actually move the jam of cars ahead of you, Prue thought, seething.

"Come on, move it, lady!" the driver, a teenager wearing a backward San Francisco Giants baseball cap, shouted at her.

Lady? Prue narrowed her eyes. Okay, she wasn't exactly eighteen, but *lady* was still on the distant horizon, thank you very much.

She wondered how Mr. Obnoxious would react if she used her powers to shake things up a little—as in, giving him a flat tire. Prue closed her eyes and rested her forehead on the steering wheel. Breathe, she coached herself. Deep down, you don't really want to do that.

It was a horrible thought, totally, Prue realized, but typical of her overtaxed mind the past few weeks. Even she had to admit it: she had been so thoroughly stressed that she'd become completely hostile toward anyone unlucky enough to cross her path. That was the main reason she was headed to the airport now—to start her week-long vacation with her sisters, Piper and Phoebe.

Phoebe, her youngest sister, had insisted that the three of them take an impromptu trip to New Orleans—the Big Easy. It would give Prue the perfect opportunity to unwind, Phoebe had insisted—to leave work and stress at home. And if Prue didn't unwind soon, Phoebe warned, things around the house were going to get ugly.

That's no idle threat when your sisters are witches like you, Prue thought. Ever since she and her sisters discovered they were the Charmed Ones, witches with the power to fight evil and protect the innocent, warlocks had been popping up everywhere. Every time Prue turned around, it seemed, some horrible creature was bent on destroying the awesome Power of Three.

Prue knew her sisters were as burnt out as she was—which was why, last night, they had made that pact: no magic while they were in New Orleans. Nothing but rest and fun. For one week, at least, they'd be three normal girls on vacation—and their vacation officially started today.

Prue clenched the steering wheel—at least it would if she ever made it to San Francisco International airport. She closed her eyes and imagined all the terrific historic sites and jazz clubs she'd visit when she got to New Orleans. . . .

If she ever got to New Orleans. "Why are you honking?" she yelled to the kid behind her, gesturing at the four lanes ahead, which had pretty much been transformed into a parking lot under the glare of the June sun. "Can't you see that nobody's going anywhere?"

He looked her in the eye and leaned on his horn again.

Wonderful. Prue rolled up her window and raised the volume on the radio to drown out the blaring sound.

She checked her reflection in the rearview mirror, running a hand through her long dark hair and examining her straight white teeth for lipstick.

She was wearing a brighter shade than usual—red, which not only matched the jacket she wore over her trim black pants, but also suited the vibrant tone of New Orleans, her destination.

"Good morning, this is Deborah Wright with your metro traffic report," said a voice on the radio. "Things sure are a mess out there on the roads this morning."

"Yeah, tell me about it, Deb," Prue muttered.

"A four-car pileup on the Bay Bridge has snarled miles of San Francisco freeway traffic. The accident is in the process of being cleared, but if you're heading over to the airport, you'd better bring along a magic carpet if you want to get there any time soon."

"Magic carpet?" Prue murmured, staring through the windshield at the lines of cars. "Hmm."

She checked the clock on the dashboard. The flight wasn't for another hour. She still had time to make it to the airport if things started moving soon . . .

Or if she used her own particular magic.

All she had to do was focus, and the traffic would be blasted out of her path. She'd have a straight shot to the bridge. Inviting, but . . .

"No way," Prue muttered, reaching for her cell phone. She and her sisters had already learned the hard way not to use their powers for personal gain. Every time they tried to use their powers solely to help themselves, the results completely backfired on them. Not that it wasn't a tempting idea ever since their grandmother died and Prue, Piper, and Phoebe discovered *The Book of Shadows* in the attic of their San Francisco Victorian house.

That was when Prue and her sisters found out they were witches, each with a special power. Now that they had joined those powers together, they were among the world's most powerful witches. It was a shame that even with all that power they still had to deal with annoying, petty stuff like traffic jams.

Prue decided to call Piper to see if she had gotten to the airport with Phoebe and to tell her what was going on. Phoebe had begged Prue not to stop into work this morning—to head straight to the airport with her and Piper instead—but Prue had to make sure everything was squared away at the auction house before she left. If Prue missed the flight, she'd just have to catch the next one and meet them in the Big Easy.

She pressed the Power button on her cell phone and started punching in the number. She frowned, realizing that nothing was happening.

"Oh, great." A flashing red light indicated that the battery was low. She tossed the phone onto the passenger seat.

Perfect, she thought. Just perfect.

"Okay, now I'm worried," Piper said, checking her watch for the hundredth time and glancing nervously down the airport corridor. Still no Prue.

"She probably got here early and already checked in. Maybe she's having coffee in the snack bar or something," Phoebe suggested. "You know Prue. She's never late."

"*We* got here early," Piper reminded her. "You complained the entire way to the airport about how I wouldn't let you hit the snooze alarm one more time." She paced to the window to look out at the plane that was connected to the gate by a jetway. The baggage handlers scurried around below, loading the cargo hold.

"Well, maybe Prue got here *earlier*."

"No way. She was going to Buckland's, remember? Besides, if she were at the airport, she'd be standing right here with us." Piper tapped her foot. "They're going to board our flight any second."

"Well, how about that." Phoebe smirked a little. "Prue's totally late while I am not only here on time, but I've made all the arrangements and reservations. In fact, if it wasn't for me, we wouldn't have gotten that great room rate at the hotel—"

"Which," Piper pointed out, "you got by agreeing to go out on the town with the guy who answered the phone."

"So?" Phoebe shrugged. "He sounded like a Brad Pitt look-alike."

"How can you tell from his voice?"

"Trust me, I can tell. And if he's not a total hottie, I'll just avoid him."

The PA system squealed briefly, and the female gate attendant's voice came over the speaker. "Standby passenger Gabrielle Toussaint, please report to the gate."

"Oh, no!" Piper watched as a pretty young woman with long, wavy dark hair hurried toward the counter.

"What's wrong?" Phoebe asked, taking a piece of gum from her pocket and popping it into her mouth.

"They're calling standby passengers. But just a few minutes ago they announced that the flight was full," Piper said grimly.

"So?" Phoebe shrugged.

"So that means that woman is getting Prue's seat."

"I'm here! Wait!" a voice called from the far end of the terminal. Piper turned. Prue!

Phoebe gestured toward the young woman who was about to speak with the attendant. "Piper, do something, or only two of us are going to be on this flight!"

Piper quickly raised her arms.

Abruptly, time stood still.

All around them, people froze in midaction, silently poised like mannequins. Only the Halliwell sisters were unaffected by Piper's time-freeze spell.

Prue raced over to her sisters. "What's with the freeze? Was the plane about to take off?"

"She was about to get your seat." Piper pointed toward the dark-haired woman who was two steps away from the counter, her mouth open and her expression expectant. "Hurry."

"I'm there." Prue scurried past the other woman and set her ticket in front of the gate attendant just as the time freeze wore off.

Piper watched as the attendant glanced, puzzled, down at the ticket, then up at Prue, who said something with a calm, cool smile. The attendant pulled apart her ticket, stapled something to it, handed it back, and then reached for her microphone again to announce that preboarding of flight 159 to New Orleans would begin.

"Uh-oh, look." Phoebe nudged Piper. "Gabrielle whatever-her-name-is doesn't look very happy, does she?"

"Happy? She's pretty much foaming at the mouth," Piper observed, stepping closer so that she could hear what was going on.

The gate attendant's expression remained the epitome of calm. "I'm sorry, ma'am," she was saying, "but I was mistaken. There is no empty seat on this flight."

"But you just called my name!" Gabrielle reminded her.

The woman scanned her list. "I'm sorry. All of the passengers have checked in. I apologize for the confusion, but I'm afraid there are no available seats."

"Well, then, find one," the young woman insisted, a warning gleam in her wide-set blue eyes. "I need to get on this flight."

"I'm sorry, but we can't just create an empty seat," the attendant explained. She turned to the microphone next to her. "We will now board passengers with tickets in rows thirty-five to twenty-five," she announced.

Piper figured that would be the end of the

argument, but she was wrong. The young woman was not backing off. "I demand that you do something about this!" she shouted.

"Ma'am—"

"This is unacceptable! You can't tell a person she has a seat—"

"I understand your frustration, but—" the attendant said.

"And then take it away for no reason," the woman ranted on. "I demand an explanation. And I'm getting on that plane. Do you understand me? Do you?"

"Gee, I sure hope she's had all her shots," Phoebe said under her breath.

"I feel sorry for the poor gate attendant," Piper whispered back.

Gabrielle Toussaint whirled around, turning on Prue. "And you!" she spat, pointing a finger. "How dare you think you can just show up and steal my seat!"

"I don't know what you're talking about," Prue said frostily. "I didn't steal anybody's seat."

"They were about to let me on board until you showed up out of nowhere."

This whole scene was starting to make Piper nervous. The last thing they needed was for Gabrielle to go after Prue and for Prue to decide to defend herself in her present stressed-out state.

"Come on, Prue," Piper said in a low voice, putting her hand on her sister's arm. "Let's get on the plane."

The three sisters made their way toward the jetway. Piper glanced back over her shoulder and saw that Gabrielle Toussaint had gone back to yelling at the gate attendant.

"She's really furious," Piper said.

"Totally over the top," Phoebe agreed.

"Forget it." Prue shrugged. "We're going to the Big Easy. No stress, no cell phones, and definitely no magic. From here on in, all we have to do is relax."

"Ladies and gentlemen, in final preparation for landing, please see that your tray tables are locked and your seats are in the upright position. We expect to be on the ground in New Orleans in just a few minutes."

"Yeah, well, it's about time," Phoebe muttered to the elderly woman next to her. "I thought we were going to circle forever."

"Well, thunderstorms, you know. Happens a lot down this way," the woman drawled.

"We're two hours late, though," Phoebe said, bouncing a little in her seat as she looked out the window at the ground looming below. "I just want to get there already."

"You and your sisters will love it," the woman assured her. "Everyone does. There's no place like New Orleans if you're looking for a good time."

Phoebe glanced across the aisle at Prue and Piper. Prue had her head buried in some dull-looking book titled, *New Orleans: A History*. Piper was dozing next to her, a Remy Fortier cookbook on her lap.

Piper's main purpose in going to New Orleans was to meet Remy Fortier, the famous Creole chef. Piper hoped she'd be able to discuss Remy's world-famous recipes with him and maybe find out his secret to a perfect gumbo. Prue, who was a history and architecture buff, was really into going to museums, the genteel Garden District, and the old slave market to learn about the city's past.

Still, Phoebe knew the Halliwells would have fun together. It would just be up to her to make sure that in addition to experiencing museums and fine New Orleans cuisine, they got to take a wild swamp tour, go to lots of clubs, and do some serious partying. After all, New Orleans was supposed to be *the* party city.

"Ladies and gentlemen, welcome to New Orleans International Airport. Please remain seated until the aircraft has come to a complete stop and the Fasten Seat Belt sign has been turned off."

Phoebe looked out the window and saw the sky was overcast. Raindrops spattered the glass. It was midafternoon local time, but from the gray look of things, it might as well have been dusk.

"Have a nice stay, dear," the elderly woman said as they made their way out of the plane. "I'm sure you'll have a wonderful time. New Orleans is just magical. Bye now."

Magical? Phoebe thought. If there's one thing I'm not interested in this week, it's magic. She shook her head, grinning.

"We're two hours late," Prue said worriedly as they waited at baggage claim a few minutes later. "What if our taxi isn't here?"

"Chill, Prue," Phoebe said, scanning the rotating carousel for her navy duffel bag. "This is your vacation, remember? I made all the arrangements. The hotel promised the taxi would be waiting."

"Well, did you ask them how long it would wait if the flight was late?"

"No, but I'm sure it'll be there." Phoebe *was* sure, which was why she was so utterly shocked when it wasn't.

"Okay, Phoebe, what now?" Prue asked, weighed down with two heavy bags over her shoulders.

"Let's call the hotel to find out what's going on," Phoebe said, heading toward a nearby bank of pay phones.

Piper lagged behind, pulling her wheeled suitcase. It weighed a ton, Phoebe knew. She was the one who had lifted it into the car earlier.

Phoebe handed Prue the number, which she'd had the foresight to scribble down and stick into her pocket before leaving home. "You do it."

"Okay." Prue took the piece of paper.

Piper rolled her bag over and plunked down on top of it. Phoebe joined her as Prue punched in the phone number.

"I'm already exhausted, and we just got here," Piper told Phoebe.

"That's because you're lugging that huge bag around," Phoebe said. "I mean, you packed enough clothes to last till next Mardi Gras."

"Well, it's a good thing I did, because you're probably going to be borrowing them," Piper shot back, eying Phoebe's lightweight duffel. "I know you, Phoebe. All you packed was a T-shirt, a pair of shorts, a bathing suit, and a toothbrush."

"Hey, I'm on vacation. What more do I need?" Phoebe asked, trying to remember if she had actually packed her toothbrush.

"Shh!" Prue said, waving her hand. She held the receiver to her ear and frowned. "What do you mean, you have no record?"

"Uh-oh," Piper said, giving Phoebe a look. "That can't be good."

"Well, can you check again? It's Halliwell, H— Yes, I know I've already spelled it," Prue said impatiently. "And yes, I know you've already checked, but please check again. It has to be there." Phoebe's heart sank as her oldest sister scowled, first into the phone and then—after hanging up—at her.

"They have no record of a reservation for us," Prue said.

"For the taxi?" Phoebe asked hopefully.

"For the *rooms*," Prue replied grouchily, frowning at her younger sister. "Did you ever confirm the reservation?"

"No," Phoebe admitted. "But it's no big deal, you guys," she added hurriedly. "We can just get a different room."

Prue sighed. "The hotel is booked, Phoebe. There's a huge baseball card collectors' convention in town."

"So? We'll try a different hotel. I didn't really want to stay over by the Superdome anyway."

"We'll be lucky if we find a room anywhere," Prue said.

Trust Prue to take the positive approach, Phoebe thought. "Oh, come on," she said, refusing to panic. "This is a huge city. There are dozens of hotels." She plucked three brochures from a nearby stand labeled New Orleans Accommodations, and handed one to each of her sisters. "Let's just start dialing."

An hour later, they looked at one another wearily. They had called every hotel in New Orleans. There wasn't a single available room to be found.

"Don't look at me like that, you guys," Phoebe said. "It's not as bad as it seems."

"Yes, it is," Piper moaned. "We're in a strange city."

"And we're completely stranded," Prue added.

"Hey," Phoebe said brightly, "maybe we can use our powers to—"

"No!" Piper and Prue cut her off in unison.

"We can't use our magic for our own gain. You know that," Prue said.

"And we promised each other, no magic while we're on vacation, remember?" Piper added.

"Well, we won't be on vacation for long if we have to leave because we have nowhere to stay," Phoebe grumbled.

"Look at the bright side," Piper said with a thin smile. "This situation can't get any worse."

"Oh, good, you're still here!" a voice called from across the baggage carousel.

Phoebe saw a familiar figure with long, dark wavy hair striding toward them. "Guys," she said. "I think it just did."

CHAPTER

2

Prue turned around to see a strikingly pretty young woman with long dark hair. Great. The lunatic from San Francisco International. She glanced at her sisters, both of whom had narrowed their eyes warily at Gabrielle Toussaint.

"Should we make a run for it?" Piper muttered under her breath.

"Oh, come on," Prue said. "She's not going to do anything to us."

"Yeah, and if she tries, it's one against three—the Power of Three," Phoebe added as Gabrielle hurried toward them.

"I'm so glad I caught you," the young woman said in her melodious accent. "I just got in on the flight that left after yours. I thought you'd be long gone by now."

16

Prue blinked. So the young woman wasn't going to have a screaming fit this time around? Talk about a mood swing.

"We would have been gone by now," Prue said carefully, still bracing herself for a scene, "but our flight was two hours late. We had to circle."

"My name is Gabrielle Toussaint," the young woman said, "and I feel awful about what happened back in San Francisco. I sort of overreacted when I didn't get on standby. I'm sorry."

"No big deal," Prue told her, not wanting to get involved. She wasn't sure which was the real Gabrielle—the shrew in San Francisco or her good twin here—and she wasn't really interested in finding out.

"I was anxious to get home because of some family problems," Gabrielle explained. "But listen, I'd like to make my little snit up to you while you're here."

"That's really not necessary," Prue began.

"Besides," Piper put in, "we're taking the next flight back home."

"What? Why?" Gabrielle asked.

"Because there was a mix-up with our hotel reservations," Phoebe spoke up. "I made them—but the hotel lost them, and now there's some big convention in town, and we can't get a room anywhere else in New Orleans. End of vacation."

"So you're leaving?" Gabrielle said. "You shouldn't have to give up your vacation. If you don't mind staying outside of the city, I know a great place that I'm sure has rooms available."

"How far outside the city are we talking about?" Prue asked cautiously.

"Not far at all. My friends Kane and Daphne Montague run a bed-and-breakfast on the bayou over in Albertine Parish. They've renovated a beautiful old plantation house. Please, let me call them for you."

"We don't want to be any trouble—" Prue began.

"Don't be ridiculous," Gabrielle said with a wave of her hand. She walked over to a pay phone.

Prue watched her with mixed feelings. She didn't trust Gabrielle. Yet staying in an old plantation house could be amazing. Besides, she hated having to end her vacation before it even began.

"All set!" Gabrielle announced a few minutes later. She was scribbling something on a piece of paper as she spoke. "Three rooms at the Montague House, ready and waiting. The only thing is, it's too far out for public transport. Can you rent a car? These are the directions."

Prue scanned the directions quickly. "No problem," she said. She gave Gabrielle a grateful smile, feeling guilty for her earlier uncharitable thoughts. "Thank you. You just saved our vacation. We really owe you for this."

"You don't owe me," Gabrielle told them. "It's just southern hospitality. You'll find a lot of that here in Louisiana."

"Well, at least let us take you to dinner," Piper said. "At Remy's. Have you ever been there?"

"Yeah, and it's incredible," Gabrielle said with a grin. "All right, we'll go to dinner at Remy's."

"How can we reach you?" Prue asked.

Gabrielle opened her brown leather bag and took out a business card. "Here, this is where I am most of the time. Just give me a call at work, and we'll make plans. And now, excuse me, but I've got to run." Gabrielle dashed for the exit.

"How cool is she?" Phoebe exclaimed.

"See? Everything is going to work out after all—even without magic," Piper pointed out.

Prue stared at the business card Gabrielle had placed in her hand. "Maybe not totally without magic," she commented.

"What do you mean?" Piper asked.

"Talk about a coincidence . . . look where she works." Prue held the card up to her sisters and pointed at the words: Jackson Square Voodoo Museum. Gabrielle Toussaint, Curator.

"Are you sure this is the right road?" Prue asked her sisters, wiping a trickle of sweat from her brow as she steered the rental car onto a narrow paved lane.

She was grateful that the rain had stopped and the sun had come out. At first they had passed wide, open fields of rice and sugarcane. But now, in the depths of the bayou, the road was dappled with shade, lined on both sides with a dense growth of shrubs, vines, and low-hanging moss-draped trees.

"This is definitely the right road," Phoebe said from the passenger seat beside her.

"Phoebe, let me see the map," Piper called from the backseat.

"Why? Don't you trust me?" Phoebe said, but handed it over anyway.

Prue sighed and reached over to adjust the air-conditioning. It was on full blast, yet the inside of the car still felt as though you could roast a chicken in it.

That's what you get for visiting Louisiana in June, she told herself. You'd think I'd be enjoying the change from all those chilly summer days in the Bay Area.

"Hey, wait! Turn there, Prue!" Piper called out suddenly.

"Where?" Prue hit the brakes, checking the rearview mirror to make sure nobody was behind her. There wasn't another car in sight and hadn't been, she realized uneasily, for miles now. Quaint local color was one thing, but just how far from civilization were they headed?

"There," Phoebe said, pointing. "At the sign that says Gaspard. That's the town we're headed for."

Prue turned onto an even narrower, shadier road marked by a small, white, arrow-shaped sign with peeling paint. The word *Gaspard* was barely visible.

"Inviting," Prue commented dryly. Minutes later the trees opened up, and they found themselves passing a few dilapidated wooden houses set on pilings.

"The stilts are to keep them from being flooded when the waters of the bayou rise," Phoebe informed them, reading from a guidebook. "You don't think the inn is going to look like that, do you? You know, all . . . crummy?"

"Maybe it's Gabrielle's way of getting back at us," Piper said darkly. "By sending us to a dump."

They passed a cluster of buildings that housed a gas station, a convenience store, and a combination town hall and post office that was little more than a shack with a flag out front.

"Was that the town?" Prue asked, slowing as they reached a fork in the road.

"That was it," Phoebe said, consulting the directions Gabrielle had scribbled for them. "You're supposed to bear left at the fork."

"But that's a dirt road," Prue said doubtfully, peering ahead.

"That's what the directions say," Phoebe informed her.

Prue steered slowly over the rutted lane. After a few minutes of driving, she muttered, "This can't be right."

They hit a jarring bump.

"I have a bad feeling, guys," Phoebe announced suddenly, sitting up straighter in her seat. "You really should have let me bring *The Book of Shadows.*"

"No way," Prue said, shaking her head firmly. "It's totally irreplaceable. We can't just go around lugging it on planes and leaving it in hotels. We have to keep it safe, and that means leaving it at home."

"Besides, for the twenty-millionth time today, we're on vacation from everything. *Including magic,*" Piper reminded them. "The last thing we want is to get tangled up with some evil warlock when we're trying to have a peaceful vacation."

"I know," Phoebe said, "but I would just feel safer if we had the book. That way, if we needed a spell, we'd have it."

"We've already gotten along fine here without any spells—thanks to Gabrielle," Piper told her.

"Hey, what's that?" Phoebe asked.

Prue followed her pointing finger and saw a gracious old plantation house set back from the road, through a grove of trees. She gasped at the sight.

The sprawling home had white pillars, lots of tall, shuttered windows, and wide wraparound porches with wrought iron railings on the first and second stories. The sweeping green lawn was dotted with magnificent old oaks dripping with Spanish moss, and gardens blooming with exotic, bright-colored flowers.

Phoebe shook her head in amazement. "That can't possibly be—"

"It is! It's the Montague House!" Prue exclaimed, spotting a hand-lettered sign hanging from a post at the foot of a curving drive leading to the house.

"It's gorgeous," Piper gasped.

"This could be all right," Prue admitted. She turned off the car and opened her door. Instantly she was hit by a wall of steamy air. "Wow, I guess the car's air-conditioning must have been working after all," she said, getting out and stretching. "It's hot out here."

"I'm sure the rooms will be air-conditioned," Piper said, as they took their luggage out of the trunk.

"What do you think, Phoebs?" Prue asked.

"It's . . . nice," Phoebe said, eyeing the building warily.

Whatever, Prue thought. She picked up her bag and led the way up the front steps as her sisters followed. She noted the red tile floor; the hanging pots of flowers; the quaint, antique, green wicker rocking chairs. The place was positively charming, and they hadn't even gotten inside yet. She couldn't wait to see the rooms; they were probably gorgeous.

She rang the old-fashioned bell by pulling a thick rope hanging from a hole in the doorframe. The door was instantly thrown open by one of the best-looking guys Prue had ever seen.

Wow. Talk about gorgeous, she thought wryly. He was broad-shouldered, muscular, and bare-chested, with sun-bleached hair and a deep tan. Prue noticed that a tool belt hung around the waist of his faded jeans.

"I saw him first," Phoebe muttered.

"You wish," Piper said through her brightest, toothiest smile.

"Are . . . are you Kane Montague?" Piper asked in an unnaturally shy voice.

He laughed. "No, I'm Randy Claudel. I'm the gardener and the handyman. The Montagues have been renovating this place, and I've been helping with the renovation. Come on in. Kane and Daphne are waiting for you in the library."

Prue smiled. Things were definitely looking up if this guy was going to be hanging around the premises.

She exchanged a glance with her sisters as they stepped over the threshold into a pleasantly cool foyer. She knew they were all thinking the same thing: Randy Claudel was a babe.

He led them toward double French doors beside a wide, curving staircase. Prue looked around appreciatively. The place was beautiful. A wide-planked hardwood floor shone beneath their feet. The afternoon sun streamed through paned floor-to-ceiling windows hung with swags of dark green brocade. The rooms were furnished in period antiques—authentic, Prue noted with a practiced eye. Gracious potted palms sat everywhere, their fronds rustling gently in the breeze from the large ceiling fans overhead.

"Kane? Daphne?" Randy rapped lightly on a glass door, which stood ajar. "Your guests are here."

"Come in," a female voice said.

Prue and her sisters stepped into a large room. The moldings were painted white; the walls were papered in red and lined with white bookcases. There were several antique sofas, chairs, tables, and lamps, and an enormous mahogany desk sat in one corner, facing a wide window that looked out on a garden.

"Hello, ladies. I'm Kane Montague," a deep voice announced.

Prue dragged her attention from a breathtaking Impressionist painting—an original, unless she was mistaken—to the middle-aged man who stood before them. He was even taller than Randy, but very thin—gaunt, really. He had black eyes and a balding patch of black hair.

"And I'm Daphne," drawled the woman beside him. She was a pretty, petite redhead with a stylish short haircut and an expertly made-up face.

Prue introduced herself and her sisters.

Then Randy, who had been hovering in the doorway, said, "If you need anything while you're here, just call," before vanishing into the hall again.

"He seems . . . nice," Phoebe said awkwardly.

Daphne Montague laughed. "Are you sure 'nice' is the word you were looking for?"

Phoebe grinned. A flush of pink colored her cheeks.

Daphne gave a good-natured laugh. "Believe me," Daphne said, "you're not the first female guest who's noticed Randy. He certainly has a way with women."

"We were just having iced tea." Kane spoke with an accent that Prue recognized as a deep patois, local to this part of Louisiana. She'd read in one of her guidebooks that the dialect combined an ancient French with hints of Spanish, German, and some African languages.

"A cool drink is such a pleasure in the afternoon heat," Daphne said in a more standard southern drawl, which meant, Prue guessed, that she probably wasn't a native of this area.

"Actually, it's much cooler in here than it is outdoors," Piper said, looking toward the open windows. "And you don't even have air-conditioning."

"The house was built almost two hundred years ago," Daphne said. "The walls are thick to keep out the heat. And we've installed ceiling fans in all the rooms."

"We try to maintain as authentic an experience as possible for our guests," Kane Montague told them. "But I'm sure you'll find your rooms quite comfortable. Would you like to see them now, or will you join us for a glass of iced tea?"

"Iced tea sounds perfect," Piper said quickly. "Are those fresh mint leaves in your glass?"

Daphne smiled and nodded. "You certainly know your herbs."

"I'm a chef, actually," Piper said.

"I'll just get Yvonne to bring in some more tea. She's our housekeeper and cook. She's a delight, although she does have a thick Acadian accent that takes some getting used to." Daphne went to the doorway and called, "Yvonne?"

"Acadian?" Phoebe echoed, looking at Prue.

"Cajun," Prue clarified. "Same thing."

Moments later a slightly built, apron-clad woman appeared in the doorway. She was one of those women whose age was impossible to guess. Prue figured she could be anywhere between fifty and eighty. Her skin was dark and wrinkled, but it might be more from the sun than from age, and her dark eyes were sharp and probing.

"The Halliwell sisters will be our guests this week, Yvonne. Would you be so kind as to bring them some iced tea?"

The older woman said something Prue didn't catch, then disappeared.

"What did she say?" Piper asked.

"She said she was pleased to meet you," Daphne said with a laugh.

"I could have sworn she said something about sharing the iced tea," Phoebe said.

"What she said was *cher*. C-h-e-r," Daphne spelled.

"Like the singer?" Piper asked, sounding puzzled.

Daphne laughed. "Not exactly."

"You'll be hearing that word a lot down here. It's a form of endearment," Kane explained.

Moments later Yvonne was back with the iced tea. As she handed the tall glasses around, Prue noticed her fingernails. They were long and curved and painted bloodred.

Prue had to force herself not to shudder. For some reason, Yvonne's nails reminded her of claws.

Piper sighed to herself. "Okay, whose idea was it to park the car on the other side of town?" she asked as she and her sisters stood under a street lamp, consulting a New Orleans map.

"It's not on the other side of town," Prue said. "It's a few blocks from here. Let's see, we're at Bourbon and . . ."

"St. Peter," Piper said, checking a street sign.

"And the car is this way."

"No, I thought it was the other way," Phoebe said.

Piper leaned against the lamppost, careful to stay out of the way of the jostling crowds around them. She watched a horse-drawn cart clop by, filled with whooping, sequin-clad women who were shouting something about a bachelorette party. The sidewalk was jammed with people, even though it was way past midnight. Lively Dixieland jazz spilled out from a nearby bar. Piper couldn't help tapping her sandal to the beat, even though her feet ached from the last two hours of dancing at a nearby club.

"Okay, we figured it out," Prue announced. "It's down that way."

Piper looked in the direction she was pointing. "Are you sure? That looks like an alley. A dark one."

"Yeah, but it's a direct shortcut to the car." She pointed at the map. "See?"

"Whatever," Piper said, waving the map away. "Let's go. My feet are killing me. I can't wait to sit down."

"They weren't killing you when all those guys were asking you to dance back at the club," Phoebe said as they started toward the alley.

Piper grinned. "And I'm sure they'll be just fine by tomorrow night. I told that last guy, Peter, that we'd probably be back then."

"Was he the one with the earring and the cute friend?" Phoebe wanted to know.

"Cute friend?" Prue said as they started down the shadowy alley. "Phoebe, you can't be talking about the guy with the purple sideburns."

"Yup, that's him," Phoebe said. "He's in a band. He said they opened for Counting Crows on their last tour."

"Yeah, *sure* they did." Piper peered ahead into the darkness. The alley seemed to be a dead end, leading only to a bunch of smelly garbage Dumpsters ahead. "You guys, are you sure it's a good idea for us to be—"

"Stop right there and don't turn around," a menacing male voice said behind them.

"Come to think of it, no, Piper, I'm definitely

not sure it's a good idea," Phoebe muttered as all three of them halted in their tracks.

Piper felt something hard jabbing into her back. "Hand over your wallets, ladies, and nobody will get hurt."

"No problem," Piper said, pulling her wallet out of the pocket of her jeans and blindly shoving it in the direction of the voice behind her.

Prue had started to open her purse, but the voice said, "Just give me the whole bag, lady."

"*Lady?*" Prue grumbled, handing it over. "Jeez. What is it with you guys?"

Piper noticed Phoebe hadn't moved.

Apparently, the mugger did, too. "Hey," he said, "where's your wallet?"

"I don't have a wallet," Phoebe said in a snotty voice.

"Phoebe, cool it," Piper said under her breath. This was not the time to cop an attitude.

"Just give me your cash, then," he sneered.

"I don't have any cash," Phoebe shot back.

"She doesn't," Prue spoke up. "She was buying rounds of drinks for everyone all night."

"Yeah," Piper said, "she's really careless with her money. She's always broke."

"Sure she is," the guy snarled.

"And even if I wasn't," Phoebe snapped, "I wouldn't give my money to you just because you—"

"Phoebe, he's got a gun," Piper cut in as whatever had been jabbing her in the ribs was suddenly removed.

She felt a wave of icy fear go through her as she heard a sharp click—the unmistakable sound of a gun being cocked.

Beside her, Prue whirled around and raised her arms in one sweeping motion. The mugger made a strangled cry as he was hurled into the air and slammed against a brick wall. He landed in a heap on the ground, moaning.

"Thanks, Prue," Phoebe said.

"Phoebe, why did you tell him you didn't have money? You should've just handed it over."

"No way. He never would've found it even if he'd frisked me."

"I'm not even going to ask where you've stashed it," Prue said, rolling her eyes. "Look, you guys, let's get out of here before that dirtbag recovers."

"And no shortcuts this time," Piper said. She glanced over her shoulder to make sure no one else was following them as they hurried back toward the bright lights and din of Bourbon Street. "I don't care if my feet are—"

"Oh, no!" Phoebe had stopped abruptly in front of her.

Piper slammed into her sister's back. "What's wrong?"

"Magic. Prue, you used your powers. No witchcraft on vacation, remember?"

"Phoebe, I didn't have a choice. He had a gun. You were about to be blasted away."

"I know, but you know what happens whenever we use magic," Phoebe said.

Piper nodded. "She's right. It's like a beacon for warlocks."

"You're right, but there's nothing we can do now." Prue sighed. "So much for our trouble-free vacation."

CHAPTER
3

Who is it?" Phoebe called as a knock sounded on her door the next morning. She was sprawled on the lilac-colored quilt that covered her white iron antique bed.

"Who else would it be?" Prue's voice replied.

Phoebe stood and opened the door for her sisters. They were both fully dressed, Prue wearing a short summer dress, and Piper a sleeveless top and shorts.

"You look like you just rolled out of bed," Piper said.

"I did just roll out of bed." Phoebe ran a hand over her wavy brown hair, thinking she really needed a trim. Maybe she could find a good hair salon in New Orleans and get a new look while she was here.

"Well, get dressed," Prue said. "It's almost noon."

"So? I'm on vacation," Phoebe said. "Plus, I thought we were going to lay low today after what happened last night."

"We are laying low. We're not going on that Garden District walking tour I was dying to check out, but that doesn't mean we can't explore the plantation," Prue pointed out.

Phoebe smiled. No matter what the situation, her sisters were ever intrepid.

"You missed breakfast," Piper said. "Yvonne made these amazing crepes. And Randy joined us wearing a really tight tank top." She smirked. "We tried to wake you."

Phoebe shrugged. "No biggie." She smiled at her sister's half-pretend competition with her over the hunky groundskeeper. Why did she and Piper always admire the same men? Just good taste I guess, she thought.

Piper flopped down on the antique fainting couch. She looked around at the pastel striped wallpaper, and the cream-and-lavender curtains that framed the lace-paneled balcony doors.

"Great room," she observed.

"How's yours?" Phoebe asked.

"Incredible," Piper told her. "I slept great."

Prue, seeing the duffel bag on the floor, looked exasperated. "Haven't you unpacked yet, Phoebe?"

"No rush, cher," Phoebe said with a grin. "I'll unpack later. It'll take, like, two seconds."

"Trust me, it will. She didn't bring *anything* with her," Piper told Prue.

"Unlike you, who brought *everything* she owns," Phoebe said as she pulled a clean T-shirt over her head.

"Let's go, guys," Prue said, "I want to have a look around. Kane and Daphne said we could explore."

"They may have just meant the house," Piper told her. "They probably don't want us snooping all over the place."

"We're not snooping, we're just getting the lay of the land," Phoebe said. She threw on a pair of shorts and grabbed the key to her door. "I'm just going to wash up in the bathroom, and then I'll meet you guys downstairs."

A few minutes later she caught up with her sisters. They headed for the back of the house. They passed through the kitchen and noticed a pot bubbling on the stove.

"Mmm," Piper said, sniffing the fragrant air. "I smell shrimp. And tomatoes and onions, too. Maybe it's gumbo."

"Let's taste it," Phoebe said, starting toward the stove. Her stomach was suddenly rumbling.

Piper held her back. "That's not a good idea. This isn't our kitchen."

"Yeah, well, I missed breakfast," Phoebe pointed out, dipping a ladle into the hot soup. She let it cool for a moment, then tasted it.

"Well?" Piper asked. "Was I right? Gumbo?"

"Yeah, and it's amazing," Phoebe said.

"All right, that's enough. Let's go outside," Prue said impatiently. "The back door is over there."

Phoebe reluctantly replaced the ladle and covered the pot. She'd be sure to sneak herself some more gumbo later.

The Halliwells stepped through the door and found themselves in a small cobblestone courtyard edged by blooming hedges, with an old marble fountain in the middle. They followed a path that led through the hedges and wove among the trees. Moments later they emerged in front of a cluster of small buildings.

"This used to be a kitchen," Prue said, looking into a window of the building nearest to them.

"How do you know?" Piper asked, peering over her shoulder.

"The huge fireplace, for one thing," Prue said. "In the old days of plantation life, the cooking was done away from the main house, to reduce the risk of fire and the unbearable heat."

"Here we go," Phoebe murmured, rolling her eyes.

When Prue got started talking about history, she could drone on for hours. And of course, Piper was interested in anything that had to do with kitchens and cooking, but this conversation wasn't exactly Phoebe's cup of tea.

She drifted away from her sisters, wandering around the building. It was shady back here, and quiet. She took a few steps and looked down. Why were her sneakers making squishy sounds? She saw that the ground was marshy beneath her feet.

She remembered that Daphne and Kane had said the plantation grounds were edged by the bayou. They had warned the sisters against venturing too far away from the house.

But that doesn't mean I can't explore a little, Phoebe thought, walking along the property, staying close to the row of old buildings. At the last one, she found a door standing ajar.

She pushed it open and started to poke her head inside.

"Stop!" a voice called out sharply.

Phoebe spun around. Yvonne had materialized behind her, a basket over one arm. In it were bunches of what looked like weeds.

"I was just peeking inside," Phoebe explained, relieved to see the old housekeeper. She gave her a broad grin.

"Don't," Yvonne said, not smiling back at Phoebe.

Phoebe stared. Why did Yvonne look so deadly serious?

The old cook's dark eyes gleamed. "Keep to yourself while you're here," she said, in her thick patois, "or you'll be sorry."

The old woman disappeared around the side of the building again. Phoebe stared after her.

"You'll be sorry?" What was up with that?

Okay, so maybe snooping wasn't such a great idea. But—

Phoebe grabbed the handle to close the door and gasped as a vision slammed into her head.

In it, she saw the terrified face of a young girl. Phoebe's mind was filled with the ominous sound of chanting, and then the young girl screamed in terror.

Just as suddenly as the vision had appeared, it vanished.

Phoebe stood perfectly still, shivering in the noonday heat. The ability to see visions was her special power. She ought to have been used to it by now, but it still took her by surprise and left her shaken.

She didn't know what the vision meant, but whatever it was, it wasn't good. As she hurried to find her sisters, Yvonne's suddenly ominous words echoed through her head. "You'll be sorry."

"Are you sure that's what Yvonne said?" Piper asked Phoebe as she and her sisters finished large bowls of spicy shrimp Creole over rice in the inn's formal dining room. Phoebe had that grim tone in her voice, the one Piper hated. The one that sounded like disaster was just around the corner.

"I'm telling you, Yvonne was definitely not kidding around," Phoebe insisted.

Piper held a finger to her lips, realizing anybody could overhear them. "Hey, Phoebs, keep it down," she said. She didn't want anyone overhearing their conversation.

"I wonder why she was warning you off," Prue said, lowering her own voice. "And why the threat? I mean, people who work at B&Bs don't usually make a habit of scaring off the guests."

"Speaking of which, where are the other guests?" Phoebe asked. "We're, like, the only ones in this place."

Piper shook her head. "No way. I'm sure there are people around. In fact, when Prue and I came down to breakfast Yvonne was clearing away some dirty plates. Someone was eating before us."

"Yeah, well, anyway, this whole place is starting to creep me out," Phoebe said. "And that vision . . ."

"You're sure you don't know the girl in it?" Piper asked.

"Pretty sure. Although there was something familiar about her eyes. They were this intense blue. I felt this strange kind of connection to her. Like maybe I've seen her someplace before, but not in person. Does that make sense?"

"Maybe you saw a picture of her," Prue suggested.

Phoebe hesitated. "No . . . I just don't know."

"Well, do you think the vision showed something that happened in the past, or the future?" Piper asked.

"You know how it is with my visions. Sometimes it's totally impossible to tell," Phoebe said. "This one could definitely be either."

"That's conclusive," Prue said. "Any idea at all what it means?"

"Yeah. Nothing good," Phoebe said grimly.

For a few moments they ate in silence. Piper tried to think of something to say. "You know," she began, "there's a hint of some kind of herb in this gumbo that I just can't put my finger on. What kind of greens did you say Yvonne had in that basket, Phoebe?"

"Gee, I don't know, Piper. I was too busy being terrified to notice."

"Hello, ladies," Kane Montague said from the doorway.

"Did you enjoy your lunch?" Daphne asked, coming up behind him.

Piper gave a little gasp. Had the Montagues overheard any of their conversation?

"It was wonderful, thank you," Prue told them.

"Absolutely delicious. Do you know which herbs Yvonne uses for her Creole sauce?" Piper asked.

"Yvonne never reveals her ingredients," Daphne told them. "She's very secretive about her cooking."

"How about joining us for tea or a glass of sherry?" Kane asked the sisters. "The Phillipses, our other guests, have just come back from a riverboat ride, and **they**'ll be joining us."

"Sounds great," Piper said. For some reason, the mention of other guests was reassuring. It made the B&B feel a little less remote.

But why do I suddenly need to be reassured? Piper wondered. Are Phoebe's jittery nerves rubbing off on me?

Piper reminded herself that everything was fine. She was on vacation. She was supposed to relax, and she had every intention of doing so. Phoebe had simply misunderstood Yvonne. That's all.

She pushed back her chair, stood up, and picked up her plate.

"Don't be silly, cher. Yvonne will clear the table. You're a guest," Daphne said, putting one arm around Piper's shoulders. "Come into the library. We'll have our tea and sherry in there."

She escorted them down the hall, through the foyer, and into the elegant library. As they went, Daphne kept up a running commentary about various items they passed, telling them that the slightly wavy window glass was original to the house, and that the gilt-framed oil painting at the foot of the stairs was of the original owner of the plantation, Captain Jean Montague.

"He was a Frenchman, my husband's great-great-great-great-grandfather. His family tree is quite interesting—although, I suppose any family tree fascinates those who are descendants."

Piper exchanged a glance with her sisters. She knew what they were thinking. Their own family tree was more than a little fascinating. Their powers were a legacy that had been handed down from generation to generation.

In the library Daphne introduced them to a cheerful pair of retirees, Harold and Marge Phillips. They were dressed alike in white T-shirts and plaid shorts. They finished each other's sentences and called each other "hon."

Piper instinctively liked them, and she was relieved to see that they seemed relaxed here at Montague House. They mentioned that they had enjoyed their stay and planned to come back next year.

See? Piper told herself. There's nothing strange going on around here.

Then again, the Phillipses weren't warlock magnets. So far, last night's little slipup hadn't seemed to spark any warlock activity, but between Yvonne's weird warning and Phoebe's scary vision, you never knew.

Kane joined them. "Yvonne will be bringing in the tea and sherry shortly," he announced. "So in the meantime, can I answer any questions?"

"When was the house built?" Prue asked.

"It was built in 1806 by one of my ancestors, a ship's captain who fell instantly in love with Louisiana on his first visit and never left."

"The house has remained in Kane's family ever since," Daphne added.

"My grandfather lived here until his death several years ago. We inherited it and began

restoring it, with Randy's help. He's been a god-
send. Showed up on our doorstep last year and
said he was looking for carpentry work. I hired
him on the spot."

"Has Yvonne been with you that long, Kane?"
Piper asked.

"Oh, she came with the house," he said with a
grin. "She worked for my grandfather for years.
And we sure are lucky, because her cooking is
legendary in these parts."

"You must be talking about me." Yvonne
appeared, carrying a tray that held a crystal
decanter and seven small, matching glasses, as
well as a tea service. She was smiling.

That's a lot of stuff piled on to one tray, Piper
thought. Yvonne might appear small, but she was
obviously very strong.

"I surely am speaking of you, Yvonne," Kane
said. To the others he added slyly, "Not a bit of
ego in her, is there?"

"When it comes to cooking, I tell it like it is,"
Yvonne said good-naturedly. She offered tea or
sherry to everyone in the room.

Piper chose a cup of tea. She always found it a
soothing drink.

"You *always* tell it like it is," Daphne said with
a chuckle.

"Nothing wrong with that." Harold Phillips
got to his feet and held out his hand to his wife.
"In case we don't catch up with you before we
leave, I just want to say that we won't be seeing

you again, Yvonne. Marge and I are taking off bright and early in the morning."

"Thank you for keeping us so well fed," Marge said, giving the older woman a hug.

Piper felt torn between relief at this evidence that Yvonne was hardly the frightening old crone Phoebe seemed to imagine and dismay that the inn's only other guests would be departing so soon.

That would leave Piper and her sisters alone on the premises with the Montagues, Randy, and Yvonne, unless some other guests were expected.

Phoebe caught her eye from across the room as Yvonne left. She was clearly thinking the same thing—and she looked troubled.

Her expression changed a moment later, however, when Randy walked in. He was wearing a clean pair of jeans and a navy polo shirt. No matter what he wears, Piper thought, he's absolutely gorgeous.

Randy asked Kane a question about the lawn fertilizer, then turned down Daphne's offer of a glass of sherry. Still, he lingered, chatting with Phoebe, who giggled and flirted in between gulps of the liquor, then allowed Kane to refill her glass from a different bottle he took from a cabinet in the room. He said it was his private reserve, a particularly fine bottle. And since Phoebe seemed to enjoy sherry . . .

Piper frowned as she nursed her tea, thinking Phoebe had better be careful.

Just because there had been no warlock activity today didn't mean they should let their guard down. The way Phoebe was guzzling sherry, she wasn't going to be able to look out for herself if anything happened.

Like what? Piper wondered. What could possibly happen?

Given their recent past, that wasn't a question she even wanted to consider.

Phoebe sat straight up in bed.

What was that pounding?

She looked around the shadowy, unfamiliar room. The windows were open, the curtains blowing slightly in a hint of breeze that stirred the sultry night air.

She realized that the sound was coming from outside. It was a rhythmic throbbing, almost like a muffled heartbeat, or . . .

"Drums," Phoebe whispered aloud, recognizing the sound.

Somebody was playing drums.

The strange thing was . . .

The B&B was out in the middle of nowhere, surrounded by the tangled undergrowth and dense clumps of trees that dotted the dark, murky waters of the bayou.

So who was playing drums at this hour, way out here?

It's probably a radio, she told herself as she slipped out of bed and padded across **the** floor to the French doors that led out onto the balcony. After a moment's hesitation she opened the doors and stepped outside.

The drumming was definitely coming from somewhere outside the main house, though she couldn't tell where. The night air was scented with floral blossoms from the gardens below, warm and heavy with humidity. She hugged herself, shivering in her T-shirt and striped cotton boxers although the temperature had to be hovering in the eighties.

She wasn't cold.

No, she was . . .

She didn't know *what* she was, actually. Maybe a little hung over. She'd had more of that sherry than she should have. And she couldn't shake the feeling that something wasn't quite right, and hadn't been since they'd started this vacation.

She leaned her arms on the wrought iron railing and looked at the row of darkened windows and doors lining the balcony. Prue's room was a few doors down, Piper's next door. She was sure that her sisters were asleep.

A slight breeze rustled the trees overhead, carrying with it another sound. This time it was a strange, high-pitched wailing, followed by guttural moaning. It seemed to be carried across a great distance, from a spot somewhere beyond the perimeter of trees that lined the yard below.

This was getting spooky. Phoebe's mind flashed back to Yvonne's warning: "Keep to yourself while you're here." It suddenly seemed like excellent advice. She felt woozy and weird, in no mood to figure out what was going on out there. This was definitely not the night to play detective.

Phoebe went back inside, closing and locking her door before diving into bed and pulling the covers over her head.

For a long time she lay like that.

After a while, she could no longer hear the wailing and moaning, but the blankets barely muffled the drumbeats that still pounded somewhere in the bayou.

Go to sleep, Phoebe told herself. So somebody's playing a drum in the middle of the night. So what? Back home she was used to sleeping through all sorts of city sounds. She could handle a little noise here.

Gradually she felt herself relax.

She might even have dozed off before another sound startled her. This time it was much closer. A creaking sound, like a floorboard in her room creaking from the weight of someone walking on it. She held her breath and reminded herself that this was an old house. Old houses creaked all the time. Hadn't she lived in one practically her whole life?

She heard the creaking again.

That was definitely a footstep.

She sat up and shoved the covers away from her face, just in time to see a shadowy figure coming at her. In its outstretched hand, something gleamed in the moonlight spilling through the open window.

A knife?

No, but it was a gleaming silver blade—

Someone was coming toward her with an enormous pair of shears.

Phoebe opened her mouth to scream. The figure clamped a strong hand over her mouth.

Phoebe struggled, but she was being held down. She couldn't move. She couldn't scream.

She was completely helpless.

And the pointed blades of the shears were slashing down toward her.

CHAPTER 4

Noooo!" Phoebe shrieked. She wrenched her body to the right, pulled free from her attacker's grasp, and leaped out of bed. Then she looked around.

Bright sunlight spilled through the window. Birds were chirping outside, and she could hear the reassuringly familiar hum of a lawnmower.

It was morning, and there was no one else in the room. No attacker, and no giant shears. It had all been some crazy dream.

But someone *was* outside her room, knocking on the door. "Phoebe?" Piper called.

Phoebe hurried to open it.

"Are you all right?" Piper asked.

"I just . . . I guess I had a bad dream," Phoebe said slowly.

"About what?"

"Nothing," Phoebe muttered. "What time is it?"

"I was just coming to wake you up. It's almost eight."

"Eight?" Phoebe groaned and headed back toward the bed. She walked over to the dresser and looked at herself in the mirror. There were deep shadows under her eyes, as though she hadn't slept much, or at all.

But she must have. She'd had that vivid dream about somebody attacking her with a pair of shears.

"You don't have time for a shower," Piper told her. "Prue wants to leave for the Garden District right after breakfast."

"It's okay. I took a shower before bed last night." Phoebe picked up her brush and ran it quickly through her hair, then began hunting in her overnight bag for her toothbrush.

"You might want to slick that down with some gel," Piper said, pointing.

Phoebe looked up to see her sister gesturing at a wayward lock of hair that was sticking out from the side of her face.

"It must have dried funny. It was still damp when I slept on it," she told Piper. She tucked the rebellious lock of hair behind her ear.

Again it refused to stay.

That was strange.

She always wore it that way. But now, suddenly, it was as though this particular clump of hair was too short to reach her ear. . . .

Almost as if it had been cut.

"See you downstairs," Piper said, and walked out, closing the door behind her.

Phoebe stared at her reflection in the mirror.

Again, she grabbed the wayward lock of hair and pushed it back. Again, it refused to stay behind her ear.

Last night . . .

The dream . . .

Could it possibly have been real?

Had somebody really been in her room with a pair of shears, and had the intruder used the shears to cut her hair?

Phoebe laughed out loud, telling her reflection, "Yeah, sure. Like that makes any sense. Why would anyone want my hair?"

She turned away from the mirror and hurried to get dressed.

"Wasn't that amazing?" Prue asked her sisters from the driver's seat of their rental car. The three Halliwells had just taken a tour of New Orleans' Garden District, famous for its beautiful homes and gorgeous flower beds.

The neighborhood had lived up to its reputation. It was filled with the some of the most fantastic architecture that Prue had ever seen. Nearly every style was represented—Queen Anne, Tudor, Victorian, and Mediterranean. Many of the homes dated back to the late eighteenth century, Prue had read, when new arrivals to the city built their large and beautiful homes with wrap-around porches, high ceilings, large entryways, and spectacular gardens.

"It was great, Prue," Piper said, "but, trust me, lunch is going to be the absolute best part of the day."

Prue parked the car in a public garage in the French Quarter. The three sisters walked down Royal Street, which was lined with two- and three-story buildings fronted by ornate balconies, en route to their destination, the restaurant of the famous Remy Fortier.

"The guidebook calls the grillwork iron lace," Phoebe told them, an open book in her hands. "Hey, see that cool house across the street? It's called the Brulatour House, and it was built by François Seignouret, a French wine merchant."

"Phoebs, look out," Prue said, catching her sister's arm before she walked into an old hitching post. "Better stop reading until we get where we're going."

"But there's so much to see along the way," Phoebe protested. "I don't want to miss anything."

Prue grinned—to think that Phoebe had been complaining about looking at "boring old houses" that morning. Now she was so into it.

Prue took a deep breath of the air that was scented with coffee and pastries from a nearby café and the damp, slightly fishy aroma of the Mississippi River flowing just blocks away. She felt totally happy amid the din of voices, traffic, and clopping hooves of horse-drawn carriages. On the next corner a band of street musicians played "Down by the Riverside."

"I'm starved," Piper said, a few steps ahead of them. She clutched a cookbook by Remy Fortier that she'd brought along with her. She was hoping to run into the famous chef and get his autograph.

"I'm not," Phoebe said. "My stomach is messed up today."

"I'll bet it's all that sherry you drank yesterday," Prue told her, shaking her head. "I could have told you that you shouldn't have—"

"Hey, I can hold my liquor," Phoebe cut in. "It's not—hey, whoa!" As they passed, a street juggler had fumbled and dropped several rubber balls. They went bounding around the sisters' legs.

"Okay, I was expecting colorful, but this city is a circus," Prue said, stepping carefully around a wayward ball.

"I know, isn't it the best?" Phoebe asked with a grin.

They crossed the street, stepping around a camera-toting couple pushing a double stroller, a group of young boys throwing a Frisbee back and forth, and a woman in a ruffled dress and garish makeup. Yup, Prue thought. This place is really cool.

"There it is!" Piper shrieked suddenly, breaking into a run.

Prue looked up and saw a restaurant bearing a sign that read Remy's. "Come on, Phoebs," she said, "you'll feel better after you've eaten something."

"I've already eaten something. I had a big pile of Yvonne's croquignoles this morning. Maybe I ate too many."

"Maybe." Prue, too, had chowed down on the sweet, chewy deep-fried cakes, which Kane and Daphne had said were like the beignet, another local version of a doughnut.

By the time they reached the restaurant and stepped into the fragrant, crowded, air-conditioned interior, they found Piper arguing with the maitre d'.

"What's wrong?" Prue asked, shouldering her way through the hordes of people who packed the small foyer area.

"He says there's a two-hour wait for a table," Piper wailed. "Even after we came all this way—"

"I'm sorry," the tuxedoed maitre d' said a bit haughtily, "but we're very busy. Look around you. Everyone is waiting."

"But—"

"Two hours is the best I can do."

"Let's take it. We can leave and come back," Prue suggested to her sisters.

The maitre d' shook his head. "Oh, I'm afraid not. I cannot hold a table for you if you leave."

"So you expect us to sit here for two hours?" Phoebe asked. "That's—"

"That's fine," Piper cut in hurriedly. "We can sit. We've been walking all morning. It'll be nice to have a rest—"

"No way," Phoebe told her.

"I'm with Phoebe," Prue said. "We can't waste two hours just sitting here, waiting for a table. I want to see more of the city. We'll come back tomorrow."

"But—"

"Sorry, Piper," Phoebe interrupted. "You're outvoted."

"All right," Piper said glumly.

"Why don't you make a reservation?" Prue suggested, hating to see Piper look so disappointed. "That way we'll be sure to get a table when we come back."

"We don't take reservations," the maitre d' put in.

Prue felt her patience evaporating. She was tempted to tell the maitre d' exactly what she thought of him and his reservations policy, but she knew that would only make Piper feel worse. "Look," she said, "let's grab a sandwich over in that outdoor café we passed a while ago," Prue suggested to her sisters, "and then we'll see what we should do next."

"A sandwich?" Piper muttered. "Who wants a sandwich? I had my tastebuds all set for Remy's jambalaya."

*   *   *

Five minutes later they sat at Gumbolaya Joe's, a restaurant situated right next to the Mississippi River. Even Piper had to admit that the po'boy sandwiches—proclaimed the specialty of the house by a large blackboard sign—were totally yummy. They were gigantic, made on French bread split down the middle and filled with ham and andouille, a regionally popular smoked sausage. The sandwiches were served alongside steaming cups of spicy seafood gumbo.

When they had finished eating, Prue spread her map on the table. "Let's see," she said, finding Decatur Street and pinpointing an intersection. "We're right here . . . and look, we're not far from the French market."

"What's that?" Phoebe wanted to know, looking up from her iced cappuccino.

"It's five blocks of stalls where you can buy authentic New Orleans foods," Prue began.

"And spices, too," Piper cut in excitedly. "Remy mentions one of the stalls in every cookbook he's written. He buys all his spices there. It's run by a woman named Madame La Roux. And this is where my cookbooks come in handy," she went on, thumbing through one. "Remy gives the exact location right here . . . see?"

"Let's go there first," Prue offered. She consulted the book and then the map. "It's nearby."

"A spice stall?" Phoebe asked. "Hold me back, girls. We're living it up now."

Prue grinned. "I don't think we have a choice."

She gestured toward Piper. "It's the next best thing to Remy's."

The three sisters soon found themselves in a pungent, dimly lit stall in the huge French market. Every inch of the place seemed to be crammed full, from the bunches of dried herbs hanging from the low ceilings, to the shelves crowded with bottles and tins, to the open bushels and baskets that lined all but a small portion of floor space.

A large, ruddy-faced woman with long, flame-red curly hair greeted them pleasantly.

"Are you Madame La Roux?" Piper asked. When the woman nodded, she gushed, "Oh, I've read all about you in Remy Fortier's cookbooks. Do you really know him personally?"

"But of course, cher," she said in a heavy Cajun accent.

As Piper quizzed her about Remy's favorite filé powder, Prue and Phoebe milled around, idly picking up vials and examining the contents.

"What is all this stuff?" Phoebe asked under her breath. "When Piper said spices, I was expecting cinnamon and nutmeg. I mean, what's filé powder?"

"I think it's used to thicken gumbo," Prue said. She picked up a small jar labeled Dragon's Blood Reed and showed it to Phoebe. "But on this one, your guess is as good as mine."

Phoebe grinned. "Sounds like it's for that new dark underworld fusion cuisine."

"Yeah, I'll stick with salt and pepper any day." Prue put the jar back on the shelf.

"In addition to being favored by the finest local chefs," Madame La Roux was telling Piper, "many of my spices are used in voodoo rituals. This, you see?" Prue watched with interest as she held up a small white packet. "This is jalop powder. It's made from High John the Conqueror root."

"What do you do with it?" Piper asked.

"It's used in a ritual that removes a curse. You mix it with other ingredients, and you sprinkle it on the doorstep of the cursed one."

"What about this?" Piper asked, taking a small, shriveled object from a basket on the counter.

"That's verbena root, cher. It's used in love spells. It's said to make passions rise quickly."

"Hey, Phoebe, maybe you should sprinkle some of this on Randy when we get back to the inn," Piper joked.

"No magic, remember?" Phoebe muttered under her breath, turning a sweet smile toward Madame La Roux. The old woman gave her a shrewd stare through her narrowed, heavily made-up green eyes.

"Do people actually buy this stuff for voodoo spells?" Prue asked, curious.

"Voodoo is very common in New Orleans," Madame La Roux replied with a shrug. "And," she said, leaning so close that Prue could smell her clove-scented breath, "I happen to be an expert on the subject."

"Really?" Prue pretended to be impressed. She could just imagine the woman's reaction if she discovered she was in the company of three witches who practiced real magic, not this voodoo hocus-pocus.

The woman nodded thoughtfully, watching her. Prue shifted her weight, suddenly uncomfortable. Maybe she *did* know. There was something strange about the expression in the woman's eyes.

"We should go," Phoebe said abruptly. "You know, so we can, uh, get back to the inn. It's such a long drive."

"Where are you staying?" Madame La Roux asked.

"In a town called Gaspard," Phoebe told her. "It's way out in the sticks, in Albertine County—"

"Parish," Madame La Roux corrected her.

"Right," Phoebe went on, "and it's about thirty miles—"

"I know where it is," the woman interrupted, a gleam in her green eyes. "Where are you staying in Gaspard?"

"At the Montague House," Prue said.

The woman gasped. "But . . . you can't stay there!"

"Why not?" Prue asked slowly. She glanced from her sisters' suddenly worried faces to Madame La Roux's expression of horror.

"Because," the woman said. She ran a distracted hand through her red hair, shaking her head rapidly, "everyone in New Orleans knows about the Montague House."

"Well, we're not from New Orleans," Prue reminded her. "What about it?"

"The place is evil," Madame La Roux rasped. "Pure evil."

Evil? Phoebe blinked. Her stomach gave a lurch. Had she heard Madame La Roux correctly?

"What do you mean, the Montague House is evil?" Prue asked, just as a pair of little old ladies walked into the stall.

"Hush," Madame La Roux said, holding a finger to her lips. In a low voice she said, "I'm sorry. I cannot tell you that."

"Why not?" Piper asked.

Phoebe chimed in, not caring whether the newcomers overheard, "You can't just tell us we're in trouble and not explain why."

"I have *paying* customers to attend to," Madame La Roux said pointedly and turned away to address the two women.

Prue scowled at her sisters. "I get the point. Let's go."

"We can't just go," Phoebe protested. "We have to find out what she's talking about."

Prue was already starting for the door. "Well, she's obviously not going to tell us unless we buy something."

"Which is fine, because I want to buy something," Piper said quickly. "This is where Remy shops for his ingredients. I—"

"Piper, you can find the same stuff anywhere in the French market," Prue pointed out.

"But—"

"Look, this woman's trying to scam us, thinking she can scare us into spending. Let's get out of here." Prue walked past Madame La Roux, who was showing the two women a jar filled with some kind of greenish powder.

Phoebe hesitated, looking at Piper. "Prue's probably right," she said in a low voice. "But what if Madame La Roux is telling the truth?"

"Just a moment," Madame La Roux murmured to her customers and stepped away from them. She picked up a packet from a bin on the counter and held it out to Piper. "Here, cher, buy this. Remy uses it in his shrimp étouffée," she said. "Usually I charge fifteen dollars for it, but for you, I'll make it ten, and—"

"Nope," Prue turned and intercepted the packet before it landed in Piper's outstretched hand. "We're leaving."

She put one arm around Phoebe's shoulders and the other around Piper's and escorted them out of the shop.

"Madame La Roux is full of it," she muttered, shaking her head.

"What if she's not?" Phoebe asked. She was feeling stranger and stranger about all of this. "Shouldn't we at least hear what she has to say about the Montagues? Piper was going to buy something anyway—" Phoebe stopped short. She steadied herself against a lamppost. Her stomach suddenly felt really queasy. "Guys, I don't feel so good," she said.

"You don't look so great either," Piper admitted, peering into her face.

"Hey, thanks," Phoebe quipped as Prue put the back of her hand against Phoebe's forehead. Her touch felt cold.

"You might be a little warm," Prue said. "Maybe you're coming down with something. We can go back to the B&B. It's okay."

"Yeah, you should rest, Phoebs," Piper said.

"Thanks." Phoebe smiled feebly. The idea of going back to bed sounded great at the moment. But the idea of going back to the B&B wasn't quite as comforting. She couldn't shake the memory of that strange dream she'd had about the shadowy stranger in her room, or the feeling that her hair had actually been cut. And what about her vision—the one of the terrified girl?

She hoped Prue was right about Madame La Roux's warning—that it was just baloney. But deep down, she wondered if the older woman might be right about the Montague House. What if the place *was* evil?

"Prue, isn't ginger supposed to be good for an upset stomach?" she asked abruptly. "You said Grams used to make you ginger tea when you didn't feel well."

"Yes, she did," Prue said, smiling at the fond memory.

"Well, I'm sure Madame La Roux has ginger root in her bag of tricks," Phoebe said, starting back toward the stall. "And I'm going to buy some. I'll be right back."

She hurried toward the shop as Prue protested that she should spend her money someplace else. All she wanted was to get the woman alone for a minute and ask her what she'd meant about the Montague House.

Phoebe stopped short, hearing Madame La Roux's voice as she approached the stall. "Did you just mention that you're staying at Villa Convento?"

"Why, yes," one of the woman's customers said. "It's lovely."

"It might be lovely, cher, but it's also cursed. Now, don't worry. I happen to have some jalop powder right here that will keep you safe throughout your stay."

Phoebe's mouth dropped open. Then she smiled.

So Prue was right. Madame La Roux *was* full of it. She told all the tourists that came to her store that their houses were cursed—just so she could sell a few extra spices and powders. Which meant the Montague House wasn't evil after all.

"Why didn't you get that ginger root?" Piper asked a few minutes later when Phoebe caught up with her sisters.

"She was fresh out," Phoebe said. "Let's just head back to the B&B. I'll take a nap, and I'm sure my stomach will settle down by tonight."

Unable to nap, Phoebe decided to wander downstairs to see if there was any ginger ale in the kitchen. She hadn't been kidding before— Grams really did say ginger helped settle an upset stomach.

On her way to the kitchen, she saw Kane and Daphne Montague walking toward the front door. "Phoebe, dear," Daphne drawled. "So glad to see you're up and about."

"Thanks," Phoebe responded with a smile.

"We're going for a little drive," Kane added. "We'll see you later." Kane held the front door open for Daphne, and the two of them exited the house.

Phoebe peered into the library and saw Prue there, hunched over the desk, an open book in front of her.

"Prue?"

Her sister looked up, distracted. "Did you rest?" she asked Phoebe.

"Not really. I couldn't sleep."

"How are you feeling?"

"Better," Phoebe lied. "Where's Piper?"

"I think she went outside to lie in the sun."

Phoebe went toward the back of the house, thinking she could go outside with her ginger ale and sit with Piper. She wouldn't mind working on a tan.

A pot lid clattered as she stepped over the threshold into the kitchen.

Yvonne stood at the stove, her back to the doorway. A pot bubbled on the front burner. Yvonne tossed a small bundle of sticks into the pot.

Sticks? Phoebe thought. Mmm, tasty. She made a mental note to skip breakfast tomorrow morning. Maybe Yvonne's cooking was why her stomach was so—

She froze.

Yvonne had something else in her hand. A dark brown clump of . . .

Something.

Something that looked suspiciously like Phoebe's own hair!

An involuntary gasp escaped her.

Yvonne whirled around, saw her, and promptly tossed whatever she'd been holding into the pot. She clamped the lid on and glared at Phoebe.

"What did you just put in there?" Phoebe asked, striding across the kitchen to confront her.

"I don't give out my recipes," Yvonne replied.

"I don't want a recipe!" Phoebe yelled. "I want to know why you sneaked into my room last night, and why you cut my hair!"

Yvonne's face bent into a scowl. "Foolish girl," she said, shaking her head and turning back to her bubbling pot. "You have no idea what kind of forces you are dealing with here."

Stunned, Phoebe just stared at her for a moment.

Then she turned and strode back down the hall. Piper was just coming in the front door, carrying a magazine and a bottle of sunscreen. Randy walked in behind her. The two were laughing, and Piper was flirting like crazy. Too bad Phoebe wasn't in the mood for a game of Catch the Hunk.

"What's up, Phoebs? Feeling better?" Piper asked.

"I need to talk to you and Prue. Come on." She dragged Piper toward the library.

"Catch you ladies later," Randy called.

Phoebe and Piper stepped into the red wallpapered room. "What's wrong?" Prue asked, glancing up from her book.

"That crazy old cook just threw a clump of my hair into her cauldron," Phoebe said, doing her best to keep the panic out of her voice.

"*What?*" her sisters asked in unison.

Phoebe took a deep breath and told them about her dream the night before, and how she could swear one piece of her hair was sticking out funny today, as if somebody had cut it.

"But why would anybody do that?" Prue asked.

"I didn't think anybody would, which was why I thought it was just a dream . . . until now," Phoebe said. She described the strange brew Yvonne had bubbling on the stove, and her conviction that her own hair was among the strange ingredients.

"Let me see your head," Prue said, coming over to her. She ran her fingers through Phoebe's hair. "There doesn't seem to be a clump missing."

"Trust me, there is," Phoebe said. "And Yvonne just threw it into her voodoo brew."

"Look, I use dried herbs all the time in my cooking," Piper pointed out. "The leaves and stems might look like something else to someone who didn't know what they were, but what you saw was probably a bouquet of dried herbs, Phoebe."

She considered that. Maybe Piper was right.

Phoebe bent her head, staring at the floor— anything to avoid her sisters' frustratingly calm expressions. The motion sent the wayward clump of hair she'd noticed earlier falling across her face. She tried to tuck it back behind her ear, but it wouldn't stay.

Somebody definitely cut my hair, she thought, turning abruptly and walking quickly toward the door.

"Where are you going?" Prue asked behind her.

"Back to the kitchen. I want to see exactly what Yvonne's cooking."

"Sounds like we'd better come along," Prue said, hurrying after her, with Piper following close behind.

As the three Halliwells marched into the

kitchen, Yvonne, who was just replacing the lid on the pot, looked up.

"Do you mind if I ask what you're making, Yvonne?" Prue began.

"Not at all. It's gumbo."

"Didn't you just make gumbo the other day?" Piper asked.

Yvonne laughed. "Cher, in these parts there are people who make gumbo *every* day."

"Can we take a look?" Phoebe asked.

"Of course." Yvonne reached for the lid.

Phoebe, Prue, and Piper stepped closer to the stove. Phoebe braced herself for whatever she was about to see bubbling in the pot.

Yvonne lifted the lid. The kettle was filled with . . .

"Gumbo," the three sisters said flatly, in unison.

"Looks great, Yvonne," Piper said with a weak smile.

"Sorry we bothered you," Prue added.

Phoebe left the room, feeling sicker inside than she had before. Had it all been her imagination? Was she just all worked up—too tense and spooked by her vision and Madame La Roux's warning to think rationally?

"Phoebe, where are you going?" Prue called after her.

"Back upstairs," she tossed back over her shoulder. "I think I really do need to lie down for a while."

"Phoebe, we have to get ready to go back to the city for dinner," Piper said.

"You know what? You guys can go without me. My stomach is still upset."

"Are you sure?" Prue asked.

"Positive."

Back in her room, Phoebe studied her reflection in the mirror. "They're probably talking about what a lunatic I am," she told herself glumly, lifting the wayward clump of hair and then dropping it again.

Sleep. She needed sleep. After a long nap, everything would be back to normal. It just had to be.

CHAPTER
5

I can't believe it! The line at Remy's was even bigger than it was the first time!" Piper wailed. "They wanted us to wait in that crowded foyer for three hours before they could give us a table!"

"I don't see why you're so bent on getting into that place anyway," Prue said. "Come on, let's go back to that café we ate lunch at," she suggested. "The food there was excellent."

"I'm not so sure we should," Piper said as they stepped out onto Royal Street.

The air was humid, and the early evening sun had vanished. A light rain was falling. Prue put up the hood of her rain jacket. "Why not? You said yourself that the po'boys were fantastic."

"Yeah, but Phoebe really doesn't feel well," Piper said, putting up her own hood. "She could have food poisoning, and it might be because of something she ate there."

"We all ate the same thing," Prue pointed out as they walked down the street. The rain was coming down harder now, as if it had just decided to get serious.

"Well, maybe it affected her differently."

"She probably just needs to sleep it off. Or"— Prue smiled slyly—"maybe she was just faking it. Maybe she stayed behind to flirt some more with Randy. Rack up some extra points with him while you're not around."

"That sounds like Phoebe," Piper agreed. "Look, I don't want to walk far. It's really starting to pour out, and the café's right over there. We might as well try it again."

Over steaming cups of crawfish bisque and a shared platter of succulent fried oysters, the sisters discussed their plan for the evening. They'd wanted a ride on a Mississippi riverboat, but the weather definitely wasn't cooperating.

"We can go to a museum instead," Prue suggested.

"A museum, with you?" Piper sighed. "We'll be there forever."

"You have something better to do?"

"Tour the Superdome," Piper said promptly. "I've always wanted to see it."

"It's just a big stadium," Prue said, waving away the suggestion. "Besides, I agreed to be dragged back to Remy's again. It's your turn to cooperate."

"Yeah, yeah, yeah," Piper grumbled. "What did you have in mind?"

"How about Gabrielle Toussaint's voodoo museum?" Prue suggested.

"Fine with me," Piper said, wiping her hands on a napkin and pushing back her chair. "Good thing Phoebe's not with us. The last thing she needs after her talk with Madame La Roux is to get more spooked about voodoo."

"Exactly." Prue stood and they walked to the door. "Phoebe's imagination doesn't need any more fuel."

After quickly consulting her map and Gabrielle's business card, which she had tucked into her pocket, Prue led Piper along the maze of narrow streets. Ten minutes later they were standing in front of a three-story building. Above their heads the two levels of wrought iron balconies were woven with delicate flowering vines that seemed at odds with the stormy weather and the sign bearing the words Voodoo Museum.

Prue and Piper made their way through the small Spanish-style courtyard to the door. Prue pushed open the door and found herself in a small foyer that was dimly lit by flickering candles. The furnishings were ornate eighteenth-century pieces. The Halliwells felt as if they had stumbled into somebody's house—except for the official-looking desk facing the door.

A young woman was seated there, in the

breeze of an oscillating floor fan. She was striking, with enormous brown eyes and lush, full lips. She wore a long, full-skirted blue summer dress in keeping with the room's old-fashioned theme. Her long, light brown hair was pulled back in a matching bow, with damp, wispy tendrils framing her face in the humidity.

"Are you here for a tour of the museum?" the young woman asked in a honeyed New Orleans accent.

Prue nodded. "And to say hello to Gabrielle Toussaint, if she's available."

"Oh, she's my sister," the young woman replied. It was only then that Prue noticed the resemblance. "I'm Helene Toussaint."

"I'm Prue Halliwell, and this is my sister Piper."

"Oh, you're the ones she met at the airport the other day," Helene said. "Gabrielle told me what happened. She said there were three of you, though."

"There are. Our sister, Phoebe, is back at the inn, resting," Piper told her. "Anyway, she's not very big on museums. Nightclubs are more her speed."

"Then tell her to visit Seven Tuesdays. That's the best dance club in the French Quarter. My boyfriend, Andre, bartends there. They celebrate Mardi Gras every night of the year."

"Sounds fun," Prue said. "We'll definitely tell Phoebe about it. Is Gabrielle here?"

"She's in the office on a long-distance call. I'll start your tour in the meantime."

Prue reached for her pocketbook. "Is there an admission fee?" she asked.

Helene smiled. "Not for friends of Gabrielle." She rose from the desk. "Are you interested in voodoo?" she asked, guiding the sisters toward a door.

"Yes," Prue said just as Piper said, "No."

They exchanged a glance.

"*I'm* interested," Prue said. "My sister is just along for fun."

Helene looked at Piper, who grinned. "Fun, fun, fun, that's me," she said, glaring at Prue when Helene turned her back again.

Helene led them into a large room filled with glass cases. There were more flickering candles, and the eerie atmosphere was enhanced by a creaking old fan whirling in an open window.

"Do you want me to go into the history of voodoo, or would you prefer to take the short tour?" Helene asked.

"Prue's a history buff," Piper said, leaning against the wall and folding her arms across her chest. "You might as well give us the whole story."

"You've got it." Helene flicked a wall switch, and a nearby display creaked to life. Life-size figures that were gathered around a ring of flickering fire began to move, raising and lowering their arms. The room filled with a strange chanting.

Prue knew it was nothing more than a taped soundtrack and mechanical dolls, but she felt a chill slip down her spine.

"Voodoo got its start in New Orleans in the mid- to late seventeen hundreds, with the import of slaves from the French island colonies of Martinique, Guadeloupe, and Santo Domingo," Helene told them. She added that, although the slaves formed the majority of voodoo worshipers in the years that followed, the voodoo priesthood mainly consisted of free people of color, many of them of mixed race.

"The most influential practitioners were the voodoo queens, with the male voodoo root doctors ranking second," she went on, leading them to a smaller glass case. She gestured at the mannequin inside. "This ceremonial clothing is said to have belonged to the infamous Marie Laveau."

"Who?" Piper asked.

"She was the most powerful of all the New Orleans voodoo queens in the mid-eighteen hundreds," Helene said.

Prue stepped closer to the case and looked at the figure. It had skin the color of café au lait, and wore a long yellow-and-red dress and madras kerchief tied around its forehead. The painted eyes seemed to burn into her own as she stared. Prue quickly looked away, focusing her gaze instead on a notecard attached to the case. A few lines of printed text related that the legendary voodoo queen had brought black magic out into the open, counting both aristocrats and convicted murderers among her followers.

"Marie Laveau was said to have possessed strong supernatural powers that were recognized and respected by blacks and whites alike, a common ground that was somewhat rare in nineteenth-century New Orleans," Helene told them. "People still visit her grave to contact her spirit and ask for her help."

Prue was grateful when Helene led them to another case. But as she stared at the contents—a collection of charms and amulets, along with small red flannel pouches—she felt a strange sensation sweep over her. This stuff was as real as the magic she and her sisters practiced, she realized. As real, and as potent.

"Those are gris-gris bags," Helene said. "They were left on doorsteps by voodoo practitioners who meant to do harm against the people in the house."

"What was in them?" Piper asked.

"Various things. They were usually filled with different herbs and powders, sometimes feathers or pieces of snakeskin, and sometimes nail clippings or hair."

Hair.

The word jumped out at Prue, sending a jolt through her.

She felt Piper's eyes on her and slowly turned to meet her sister's wary gaze.

"Is everything all right?" Helene looked from Piper to Prue.

"Um, of course," Prue said, and fanned the air. "It's just warm in here, that's all."

"I know. I really wish we could afford to install central air-conditioning," Helene said apologetically. "But we've only had the museum for a year, and until we get on our feet financially . . . well, the fans will have to do in the meantime."

"It's all right," Prue said. "Please go on, Helene."

Gabrielle's sister went on to tell them more about gris-gris, the New Orleans brand of voodoo. According to her, it was very different from Haitian or African types of voodoo. She showed them a case containing vials and packets that held powders and herbs used in casting spells.

"Some of these are common items that are found in most American backyards," she said, gesturing at a sprig of dried rosebuds. "Others, such as dried lizards and powdered bones, are obviously less common."

She flipped another wall switch.

The last display in the room came to life. It showed a woman in an open, thatched-roof hut. She was crouched at the base of a pole at the center, and at her feet was a red-stained circle of concrete.

"This is an *hounfort*," Helene told them. "It's a voodoo temple. The woman has been placed on the sacrificial altar."

"I take it that's not a good thing," Piper said dryly.

The mechanical figure cowered and trembled, and the soundtrack blasted her whimpers and cries, along with chanting and drumbeats.

It's not real, Prue reminded herself, staring in fascination. It's just a hokey display. So why did the mechanical woman's dread seem to fill the room?

"Why is she being sacrificed?" Piper asked.

"To satisfy the *loa*, the spirits that are summoned during voodoo ceremonies. The *Rada loa* are the kind loa, representing warmth and stability," Helene informed them. "The *Petro loa* are the dark forces who can be violent and deadly."

"And this woman is being sacrificed to a Petro loa?" Prue guessed.

Helene nodded and went on in a lower voice, almost as though she didn't want to be overheard, "Those who practice the black magic associated with the Petro loa are shunned by legitimate voodoo practitioners."

"Why?" Piper asked.

"In part because it's very dangerous. These black magic groups are called *secret sociétés* in the Cajun dialect. When a worshiper calls on any Petro loa to perform a harmful act on their behalf, they must then vow to serve that loa. This deal is called an *angajan*. If the deal is not fulfilled, vengeance will come to the worshiper."

"Sort of like your classic deal with the devil," Prue murmured.

Helene smiled. "More or less."

Prue wondered why she was so creeped out by all this stuff. It must be the soundtrack for the display, she decided. All the pounding and drumming made her uneasy. "Why is that pounding so weird and offbeat?" she asked.

"Drums are used in most voodoo ceremonies," Helene explained. "The ones honoring the Rada loa have a rhythmic pounding—unlike the erratic drumbeats used by the secret sociétés that worship the Petro loa."

As Helene stopped speaking, the soundtrack ended. "But if these dark ceremonies are held in secret," Prue asked, "how can you be sure they're real?"

"Because I—"

At that moment they heard footsteps and voices in the room behind them. "Hello. Is anyone here? Are you open?"

"More visitors," Helene said with a smile. "Would you mind terribly if I just left you on your own?"

"No problem," Prue assured her. "We'll just look around." She and Piper continued into the next room, which featured a collection of mounted, enlarged photos on the wall. Prue examined a picture of a turban-clad woman hovering a few feet above the ground.

"This place is freaky," Piper said. "All that chanting and sacrificing of goats and hens. I mean, get real."

"We chant," Prue pointed out.

"Yeah, *words*," Piper told her. "Our spells are in plain old English. And we don't beat drums."

"Does that make us any less freaky?" Prue wondered out loud. She turned to her left as she heard voices. "Is that Gabrielle?" she asked her sister.

They walked toward an open doorway off to the side of the gallery. Sure enough, Prue heard Gabrielle Toussaint's voice, but her words and tone of voice made Prue stop in her tracks.

"You followed her to a ceremony?" Gabrielle was saying. "Andre, I thought she was done with the secret société."

"So did I," a man's deep voice answered. "But you know Helene. For her, voodoo is magic and excitement. She does not believe that if she seeks out the Petro loa, they will one day tear her apart."

"But you stopped her?" Gabrielle asked.

"Yes," Andre answered. "I caught her before she reached the temple. Last night she listened to reason. But I think we will have to be careful and watch her. She is easily influenced."

"All right," Gabrielle agreed tensely.

Prue glanced at Piper as Gabrielle Toussaint walked out of her office accompanied by a tall, darkly handsome man wearing a black T-shirt and black jeans.

"Prue, Piper!" A smile lit Gabrielle's face. "I'm so glad you are here. Let me introduce you to

Andre. He is my sister Helene's fiancé. Prue and Piper are visiting from San Francisco," she explained to Andre.

"Welcome to the Big Easy," he said with a charming smile. "You must come visit Seven Tuesdays, the club where I work. Then you will see this city at its best."

Gabrielle punched him lightly on the arm. "And this museum isn't the city at its best?"

Andre grinned at her. "Only if you have a taste for the macabre. Excuse me," he said to the Halliwells. "I must find Helene. We have a dinner date tonight."

"So you've been touring the museum?" Gabrielle asked Prue.

Prue noticed that she, too, was wearing an old-fashioned costume. Her black hair was piled on her head, emphasizing her striking features and enormous dark-lashed blue eyes.

"Helene gave us the tour," Prue said. "She told us about the Petro loa and the Rada loa. It's fascinating."

Gabrielle nodded. "That's one way to describe it."

"*If* you believe in it," Piper said, shooting Prue a glance. "Your sister seems to."

"So do I," Gabrielle said. "Voodoo is real, Piper, and the secret sociétés are very dangerous."

Prue was tempted to ask Gabrielle about the conversation they'd just overheard. Was Helene involved with a secret société? she wondered. But she didn't want to confess to Gabrielle that they'd been eavesdropping.

The door in the front room opened and closed.

"Sounds like we have more visitors," Gabrielle said. "I'd better go check. Take a look around, and I'll be back in a few minutes."

She left, and they heard her talking to a group of tourists in the next room.

Prue again leaned over the glass case containing the illustrated chart of evil spirits. Some of them looked like dragons, with fire-red eyes. Others looked like angry serpents that were coiled and ready to strike. One spat bright red blood from a mouth lined with dripping fangs.

"What are you looking at?" Piper peered over her shoulder. For a long time they were silent, studying the frightening images. "You know," Piper said in a low voice. "When we first came to New Orleans, I thought voodoo was just a lot of superstitious nonsense. But the stuff in here—"

"I know," Prue said. "It's a little too real."

"Let's get out of here," Piper said finally. "I've had enough voodoo for one day."

"I was just thinking the same thing," Prue said.

In the next room the sisters said good-bye to Gabrielle, who was just starting a tour with a group of senior citizens.

"But do you have to leave so soon?" Gabrielle protested.

"We'll be in touch," Prue promised, before she

and Piper escaped into the rainy New Orleans street.

"Want to go tour the Superdome now?" Piper asked.

"Definitely," Prue agreed.

Anything to get her mind off the eerie exhibits they'd seen in the voodoo museum.

Phoebe rubbed the sleep from her eyes, opened the door to her room, and peered out into the hall of Montague House.

It was deserted. What time was it? There was no clock in her room, and she had forgotten her watch back home—not something she planned to admit to her sisters.

She had thought a nap might make her feel better, physically and emotionally, but she was just as uneasy as she had been earlier, and even more nauseated.

Maybe it was something I ate. Or maybe how much I ate. Those po'boys were big enough to choke a horse, she thought, knocking on Piper's door.

There was no answer there, nor at Prue's door. Her sisters must still be in the city—probably having a fantastic dinner at Remy's.

Phoebe descended to the first floor of the mansion, where long shadows fell through the open windows across the polished floors. All was quiet. Daphne and Kane must still be out, Phoebe thought.

Stepping outside, she saw that the sun had

almost set. It must be just past seven in the evening, Phoebe thought. She headed down the steps and across the lawn.

"Hey!" a voice called to her.

It was Randy. She noticed that he was wearing nothing more than a pair of denim shorts that revealed his tanned, muscular torso and legs. In his hand, he held a dripping hose poised over a bed of bright pink and yellow snapdragons he'd obviously been watering.

"What's up?" he called to Phoebe.

She relaxed and allowed herself to appreciate his sun-bleached blond hair and long-lashed blue eyes as she walked over to him. Okay, he was definitely a good reason to hang around Montague House, Yvonne or no Yvonne.

And Piper—a.k.a. the competition—was miles away, sightseeing.

"Hey, Randy. I'm just going for a walk," she told him.

"Well, don't wander too far," he said.

"Why not?"

"There are snakes and gators back there," Randy said with a shrug, gesturing at the heavy vegetation that bordered the property. "Wouldn't want you to become a snack for one of our scaly friends." He paused. "I'm sure they'd recognize you as a sweet treat almost instantly."

Phoebe's face grew warm at the compliment. She stepped closer to Randy. "You know a lot about this place," Phoebe said.

"I should. I live here."

"You do?" Surprised, she asked, "Where's your room?"

"Oh, it's not in the main house. That's just for the Montagues and their guests. I have one of the cabins out back. It used to be an old laundry. Yvonne has an apartment in what used to be the carriage house—it's that brick building at the back of the property."

"Really? I didn't see a carriage house."

"I'll show you where it is. Just give me a second to put away the hose," he said, coiling the green tubing in his hand.

They made their way around to the back of the main house, and Randy wound the hose onto its holder in the courtyard. He told her about the native flowers that bloomed in the bright-colored beds. Phoebe wasn't much of a gardener—okay, she didn't know a petunia from a poppy—but she acted as if she knew what he was talking about.

If she played her cards right, maybe she should see if Randy was into checking out a club later tonight. Her stomach was sure to be better by then.

"That's the carriage house back there," he said, gesturing at a two-story brick structure almost concealed by a stand of moss-shrouded oak trees. "My cabin is over there."

She followed the direction he was pointing in and saw the cluster of small buildings she and her sisters had explored yesterday, before Yvonne had shown up with one of her cryptic warnings. She wondered if she should tell Randy what the cook had said.

He was a stranger, but maybe she could trust him. She certainly *wanted* to trust him.

"Would you like to see the old cemetery?" he asked.

A chill went through her. "Cemetery?" she echoed.

"New Orleans is famous for its cemeteries," Randy went on. "People who could afford it had raised tombs constructed. Back when this place was a working plantation, the Montague family used to bury their own right here on the property. That's where I'm taking you."

"Sounds . . . interesting," Phoebe said. Okay, so Randy was into cemeteries. There were weirder hobbies, right?

"The tombs are beautiful and elaborate, and the stones are carved into statues. My favorite of all is a winged angel for the grave of a young girl." Randy's blue eyes took on a faraway expression.

"A young girl?" Phoebe echoed. "How did she die?"

"Who knows?" Randy asked with a shrug, turning his face away, as if he'd realized she was watching him. Maybe he didn't like anyone to see that he had a sensitive side, Phoebe thought. But it was a side she definitely liked.

The path wove through dense undergrowth,

where the dappled sun gave way to deep shade. It was swampy back here, and no wonder—they were walking only a few feet from the dark, murky waters of the bayou.

She stayed close to Randy, remembering what he'd said earlier. "So there are gators back here, huh?" she asked a little nervously. "Exactly how big—"

Her words were lost in a shriek as something suddenly slithered into her path.

It was an enormous green snake.

Phoebe felt her body go stiff with terror as the snake reared up and hissed, poised to strike.

Randy spun around, saw the snake, and swooped down over it.

As Phoebe watched, trembling, Randy grabbed the creature just beneath its head.

The snake thrashed about as Randy brought it close to his face. Then it began to quiet. Looking directly into its eyes, Randy whispered to it.

The language was like nothing Phoebe had ever heard before. She listened, transfixed, waiting for the snake to attack Randy, but in a matter of seconds it relaxed, so that it hung practically limp in his hands.

Randy bent down, then set the snake gently back on the path.

Phoebe jumped back and stifled a shriek. But the reptile slithered meekly away.

"The cemetery is this way," Randy said, gesturing ahead as though nothing had happened.

But Phoebe wasn't going anywhere. "What did you just do to that snake?" she demanded.

Randy grinned. "Something my grandfather taught me. He grew up in the bayou. He had a knack for calming critters."

"Handy talent to have," Phoebe said. But she couldn't help wondering exactly what kind of talent that was. Was it some kind of strange voodoo? Was Madame La Roux right? Did dark, dangerous magic lurk at Montague House?

They came to a fork in the path. "The cemetery's down there," Randy said, pointing to the left.

Phoebe took a step forward. "Whoa!" Her foot slipped on the marshy ground.

She grabbed Randy's sleeve to steady herself, and a vision suddenly filled her mind.

It was that girl again—that terrified blue-eyed girl she had seen in her last vision. The girl was surrounded by strange, insistent chanting. A shadow loomed over the girl, who squirmed and writhed in a desperate effort to get away. The girl screamed, and the shadow descended . . . and Phoebe saw that it was an enormous reptile, its open jaws about to close over the girl's head.

She gasped.

Randy turned around. "You okay?"

Looking at his face, she nodded mutely.

Whatever she'd just seen had something to do with Randy. She could feel it.

What had actually happened to **the** girl? Had

she really been devoured by a giant reptile? And if she had, what did Randy, the snake charmer, have to do with it?

One thing was certain. Whatever Phoebe's heart might be saying to her about Randy, Phoebe was going to have to ignore it. Being "in like" with Randy was becoming a very dangerous proposition.

CHAPTER
6

That night Piper woke up suddenly, uncertain why.

She reached out and felt around for her watch on the bedside table. Finding it, she turned the illuminated dial toward her face. It was a few minutes past midnight.

The rain must have stopped, she realized. She had drifted off to sleep an hour earlier to a steady plop of raindrops. She got out of bed and walked across the room to open the window, letting in the merest hint of a breeze. It didn't even begin to cool the thick, sultry air in the room.

Phoebe.

Piper wondered how her sister was sleeping. She went out into the hallway and knocked softly on Phoebe's closed door. No answer. She pushed it open and saw Phoebe in bed, asleep—although not soundly, it seemed, from the way her head turned from one side to the other.

Piper closed the door again. Back in her own room, she started to climb back into bed. But it's so hot, she thought, brushing sweat-dampened hair back from her forehead.

She stepped out onto her balcony.

It was a little better out here. The rain had cooled the temperature slightly, yet the air was still heavy with humidity and eerily shrouded by drifting bands of mist. She could smell the sweet fragrance of tropical flowers mixed with the smells of damp earth and dank swamp water.

Piper stared out over the yard at the murky canopy of trees lit by the low spotlights that dotted the property.

She frowned.

Something was flickering off in the distant marshland, among the trees.

She peered into the darkness.

Firelight?

That was strange.

Whoa, whoa, whoa, before you get all spooked, she told herself, stop and think.

A storm had passed through earlier. What if lightning had struck something and started a fire? Piper wondered whether she should wake the Montagues and decided against it. At least, not yet. First she'd go out and see what had caused the fire.

Maybe it was just Randy, burning brush or something.

At this time of night? her inner voice asked doubtfully. In this heat?

Still, she quickly changed into a pair of shorts, a T-shirt, and sneakers, then made her way through the silent, sleeping house. A part of her was scared. Yet another, stronger part of her needed to do this. If nothing else, then just to prove to herself that there was nothing to be afraid of.

There was absolutely no reason not to stroll out into the steamy summer night . . . was there?

She stepped out into the back courtyard, then hung back for a moment.

What is that?

She thought she'd heard some kind of pounding. It must have been her own racing heart, she realized after a moment. This was ridiculous. Her heart was hammering as though she had something real to be afraid of, and she absolutely didn't.

I probably should have brought a flashlight, she told herself.

But she quickly realized she wouldn't need one. Spotlights lit the landscaped yard, and the storm clouds overhead had given way to a full moon that cast the wisps of mist in a spooky white glow.

Piper walked across the clipped grass, heading toward the path that led into the trees behind the cluster of cabins. As she passed the last one, the pounding started up again suddenly.

She stopped, listening.

Okay, it definitely wasn't her heart—which did happen to be throbbing frantically at this point. The pounding that echoed through the night was a drumbeat—yet it had a strange rhythm. Actually, it seemed to lack a distinct rhythm.

Piper frowned, remembering something Helene had told them in the museum that afternoon.

She had said that drums were used at most voodoo ceremonies, and that the ones honoring the Rada, or beneficent loa, used a rhythmic pounding—unlike the erratic drumbeats used by the secret sociétés that worshiped the Petro loa.

The drumbeats she heard this hot June night were definitely erratic.

So maybe I should turn around and go back to my room? she asked herself. Yet she continued to move cautiously along the path, needing to prove to herself—and okay, to her sisters, too—that there was nothing to fear.

She moved quietly along the marshy ground that was even more damp than usual from the evening's rainfall. Night birds called from the trees overhead, insects chirped and whirred. Mosquitos buzzed constantly around Piper's face and ears, and she swatted at them whenever they landed.

The flickering firelight was always visible

ahead, growing closer as the drumbeats grew louder.

Then she heard the voices. A group of voices, chanting in a language she didn't understand.

Her instinct was to turn around and run back to the house as fast as she could. But she fought it. After all, she had something over whoever was chanting and beating drums in the dead of night in the middle of nowhere. They might be carrying on centuries-old superstitious rituals, but Piper had real powers. She could protect herself against . . .

Well, against anything, she thought, shoving back her misgivings as she spotted a clearing in the swamp a few yards ahead.

She slipped into the shadows at the edge of the path, moving quietly from tree to tree. As she crept closer, goose bumps formed on her arms and legs, despite the warmth of the night.

She could feel magic in the air. The drums beat on. The chant grew faster, more intense.

Swampy black muck closed over her sneakers when she stepped too close to the dank water at the edge of the path. She moved closer still, mesmerized by the sound, by the flickering firelight, by the overwhelming need to see, to know.

Now she heard the voices more clearly. One male voice rose above the rest, calling for silence. Piper took another step forward and peered around the trunk of a massive oak.

There, in the clearing ahead, she saw a circle of

figures wearing red robes and red masks. One of the taller figures raised his arms and began to speak. Though Piper didn't understand the individual words, she couldn't mistake his intent.

Powerful forces were being summoned, so palpable that she could feel the energy stirring around her.

"I call upon the société's power now, to defeat those who oppose us," the leader said, switching into English. "We call on Zdenek to bring suffering and death to our enemies." He drew a circle on the ground before him with some sort of white powder, and then began outlining an intricate figure on the ground. Piper recognized it as a vèvè, something she'd seen in the museum. A vèvè was a symbol for a loa, used to summon it.

Piper swallowed hard—she was witnessing a Petro loa ritual.

Okay, so maybe this was dangerous. Maybe she'd been wrong. Maybe she'd better get out of here—now. She turned, then stopped short, hearing a rustling in the tangled jungle of underbrush nearby.

A large creature crawled onto the path. She could see its golden eyes gleaming in the glow of the moon. It was an alligator.

For a moment she and the massive reptile stared at each other. This can't be real, Piper thought. It was something out of a B movie: City Girl Meets Swamp Creature.

The gator opened its huge jaws, revealing rows of sharp, gleaming teeth.

Okay, it's real, Piper decided. Run! a voice inside her head shrieked, and she went into motion, tearing along the uneven, spongy path.

She heard the alligator flailing along behind her.

Could she possibly outrun it? She'd heard that gators were fast, that they could outrun—

She screamed as another of the immense creatures emerged on the path in front of her. She turned frantically to get away, but the one behind her was less than a yard away. Then she realized that there were other pairs of eyes glowing in the dense thicket all around her.

She was surrounded.

The night was alive with heavy, swishing tails and lumbering footsteps. Countless pairs of predatory golden eyes were trained on her.

The gators were coming closer.

And closer.

Then she ran, as fast as she could, back toward the house. Her heart was pounding, her leg muscles burning, and there was a sharp ache in her side. The gators pursued, but she pushed herself to go farther, faster. She'd almost reached the edge of the bayou when she slammed into something—or someone.

Strong arms closed around her, and a hand clamped over her mouth. She struggled to scream.

Then, something cut through the numbing fog of terror.

A voice mumbling a stream of words—words Piper couldn't understand. She saw the glittering eyes of the gators retreat into the swamp. In a moment they were gone. "Piper," the voice said.

Randy's voice, Piper realized. She turned to see the inn's rugged blond handyman.

She wanted to sink to the ground in relief. Yet she forced herself to remain standing, uncertain whether she could trust anyone in this strange, frightening place—even Randy.

"Are you okay, Piper?"

She nodded mutely.

He removed his hand from her mouth, motioning for her to be quiet. He tilted his head, listening.

"How did you know I was out here?" she asked in a shaky voice.

"I can't explain now," he said, taking her by the arm. "But we have to get away, before—"

"Before what?" she prodded when he broke off. "Before the gators catch up with us?"

"Before the drumbeats stop," he cut in.

That was when she became aware that the irregular beat in the distance had picked up its pace and its volume. It seemed to grow frenzied as she and Randy swiftly and silently made their way along the path back to the plantation house.

Only when they had emerged onto the manicured grounds again did Randy stop running. He released her arm. "Sorry about that," he said. Piper couldn't help noticing that the moonlight gave his hair a silvery sheen. "Are you sure you're all right?" he asked.

Piper nodded, struck once again by how good-looking he was and how genuinely nice he seemed. Too bad Phoebe's got a crush on him, she thought. She could get interested in Randy herself.

He gave her a curious look. "What were you doing out in the bayou in the middle of the night?"

"What were *you* doing out?" she countered.

"I heard someone go by my cabin," he replied. He gave her a smile. "Since there's normally not much traffic at this hour, I thought I'd check it out."

"Oh," she said. Randy's answer sounded perfectly reasonable.

"Now, how about you?" he asked.

"I saw the fire and I heard the drums," she told him. She sank down on a marble bench, suddenly struck full force by the impact of what had just happened.

"What else did you see and hear?" Randy asked.

"I—I followed the sound of the drums, and I saw something that looked like a ritual. There were a bunch of people in red robes, and this man—the leader, I guess—it seemed that he was summoning something. He talked about stopping their enemies. He drew a symbol on the ground with white powder."

"You—" Randy started to say, but seemed too shaken to finish the sentence.

"What?" she asked. "What's going on? Do you know who those people were or what they were doing?"

Randy's blue eyes met hers. "What you saw was a voodoo ceremony—prayers to the Petro loa. What happened after he drew the white symbol?"

"This is going to sound unbelievable but I started to run and all these gators came after me," Piper said. "They surrounded me."

In the moonlight she saw Randy go pale. "They knew you were watching, Piper."

"The gators?" she asked, confused.

"The secret société."

"But how could they have known? They didn't see—"

"Those gators were summoned to stop you," he snapped.

"What are you saying?" she asked, staring into his grim face.

Randy stared at the ground for a long moment. When he spoke again, his voice was so quiet that Piper had to strain to hear him. "I'm saying you're in terrible danger," he began. "I'm saying they must have seen you, which means there's a good chance they'll come after you. You're in trouble and you have to leave. You have no idea what these people can do."

Her jaw dropped. "You're telling me I have to leave the inn?"

He gave her a wry smile. "Yeah, and I'll probably lose my job if the Montagues ever find out I'm encouraging their guests to bail. But this is serious, Piper. You and your sisters can't stay here now."

Piper drew back. "Wait a minute," she said. "How do *you* know what these people can do? How do you know how dangerous they are?"

He got to his feet, looking drained and tired. "That's a really long story," he said. "Just trust me on this, please."

But Piper still had more questions. "Randy—"

"Go inside," he said, turning away from her. "Go back to your room, and whatever you do, don't come out until morning."

"But—"

"Piper." His voice had suddenly gone hard. "Don't mess with what you don't understand." Then he disappeared into the darkness.

Shaken, Piper quickly made her way back toward the house. She had almost reached the courtyard when she rounded a hedge and saw somebody lurking a few yards away.

It was Yvonne, she realized.

The old woman's eyes glittered strangely in her weathered face.

"Hi." Piper sidled her way over to the door.

"You shouldn't be out here now," the older woman told her in an ominous tone.

No kidding, Piper thought.

She glared at Yvonne. By the way, you didn't happen to be dancing around a fire in a red mask just a little while ago, did you? she wondered silently.

"Foolish tourists." The older woman shook her head and walked away, disappearing into the shadows.

Still trembling, Piper slipped into the house, closed the door and locked it behind her, then leaned against it. Her heart was racing, her mouth dry.

Something weird was definitely going down in the bayou. She had to wake Prue and Phoebe and tell them what she'd seen.

Prue heard somebody calling her name from across a vast distance.

"Go away," she murmured, rolling onto her stomach. She was tired. So tired.

"Prue!"

She opened her eyes. That time the voice had hollered in her ear. She saw Piper standing over her bed, dressed in a T-shirt and shorts.

"Is it morning already?" She glanced at the window and saw that it was dark out.

"No, but I need to talk to you, and this can't wait."

"What's wrong?" Prue rubbed her eyes, then noticed Phoebe standing behind Piper. She was dressed in her rumpled T-shirt and boxers, making no effort to hide a huge yawn. Obviously Piper had woken up their younger sister as well.

"Close the door, Phoebe," Piper instructed.

Phoebe closed the door, then sat on the end of Prue's bed.

Piper paced over to the window. Prue could tell that she was upset about something.

Piper cleared her throat. "I woke up around midnight. I heard drumbeats and saw a fire burning in the swamp," she reported.

"I heard drumbeats the other night, too," Phoebe put in, "but I decided not to find out where they were coming from."

"Yeah, well, I wish I had been that smart," Piper said.

Prue listened as Piper told them how she had gone out into the bayou to investigate, and described the weird ritual she had witnessed. Then she told them about the alligators that had closed in on her and how Randy had shown up out of nowhere, mumbled something in another language that made the alligators turn tail—then warned her, warned them all, to leave.

"Whoa!" Phoebe breathed.

"What is it?" Prue asked.

"Seems alligators aren't the only reptiles who speak Randy's language." She took a deep breath. "I took a walk at about seven, and Randy was finishing up watering. So he and I started walking together."

Prue sat up. This was getting interesting. She

knew Phoebe had a bit of a thing for Randy. Now the two of them were taking walks together, and Randy seemed to be acting rather suspiciously. It smelled like trouble.

"And?" Prue prodded.

"And Randy grabbed the snake and started whispering to it in some weird language. The next thing I knew, the snake slithered away."

"Okay—so the guy has a way with wild creatures, and he likes to take walks in the bayou at night," Prue said, wanting to be logical. "Just because he managed to calm a snake doesn't mean—"

"There's more," Phoebe said. "After the snake-charming bit, I grabbed Randy's arm. I had a vision. It was of a young girl, trying desperately to get away from a giant reptile. The same young girl I saw before when we first arrived here. And I don't know how, but that vision was connected to Randy. I'm sure of it."

Piper shuddered. "I don't like this one bit." She rubbed her arms. "Well, we know we can't trust Randy. I mean, what was he doing out so late at night? How did he know so much about what was going on out there in the bayou?" She paused. "What if he was one of those people in the red masks?"

Prue stood and paced the floor. "Or," she offered, "what if he's a warlock?"

"No way," Phoebe said. She glanced at Piper. "Do you think he is?"

Prue shrugged. "We can't be sure. If he is part of that cult, or whatever it was that Piper saw, then we ought to get as far away from him as we can. Ditto if he's a warlock. And if he's neither—if he's actually a good guy—then we probably ought to take his warning seriously."

"I agree." Piper nodded. "There was something really dark being called up at that ceremony. Somehow, I could feel it."

Phoebe moaned and sat down on the bed. She placed a hand lightly on her stomach. "So that settles it. As long as this bod cooperates, we're out of here first thing in the morning."

Piper frowned. "Are you still not feeling well?"

"Terrible." Phoebe plopped her head down on Prue's pillow. "But I'll be okay in the morning. I'm sure of it."

Prue continued to pace. "What I don't get," she said at last, "is why this cult would want to harm us. We didn't do anything to them. They don't know us. It doesn't make sense."

"Maybe they know *about* us," Phoebe said in a low voice. "That we're . . . charmed."

"But how could anyone know?" Prue asked, shaking her head.

"The mugger in the alley," Phoebe answered. "You used your power against him. Maybe some warlock or cult member or something picked up our little supernatural blip on their radar."

Prue thought about it. "That's possible, I

guess. But this ritual—do you think it was actually aimed at us?"

"I'm not sure," Piper said. "I mean, we're in voodoo country. It's possible they were just having one of your run-of-the-mill Petro loa rituals. But if Randy's right, then they saw me, and that could have put us all in major trouble."

"I wonder if we should ask the Montagues about this," Prue mused.

"Who says we can trust *them?*" Phoebe's voice sounded muffled as she spoke through the pillow.

"That's right," Piper said. "Someone was out in that swamp wearing masks. We don't know who's involved. Girls, whether Randy's on our side or not, I think we should listen to him and get out of here. We'll find somewhere else—someplace safer—to stay. Then we'll spy on this cult to find out what they're really up to."

"What if we can't find another place to stay?" Prue asked.

"Then we go home," Piper stated. "I don't know about you but I don't feel comfortable closing my eyes, knowing that someone is summoning evil spirits in my backyard."

"I agree," Phoebe said. A look of sadness crossed her face.

Prue gazed sympathetically at her sister. Phoebe's eyes seemed kind of sunken. Not only might she and her sisters be in danger, one-third of their Power of Three seemed to be functioning

at half speed. Prue made up her mind. "Okay,"
she said. "You guys are right. We shouldn't take
any chances. We, of all people, know better than
to play around with magic."

Phoebe and Piper sighed in relief.

"Some vacation, huh?" Piper said, plopping
on the bed next to Phoebe. Prue squeezed in
between her sisters.

"It's okay," Phoebe said, snuggling under the
sheet. "We'll come back to New Orleans again
someday."

"Know what, Prue?" Piper asked, yawning.

"Hmm?"

"I'm going to fall asleep right here."

"Me too," Phoebe said with a yawn.

"It's okay, guys. Stay." Prue pulled the sheets
up over Piper. "I'll crash on the rocking chair by
the window. It's safer for us to be together right
now, anyway."

CHAPTER 7

Phoebe opened her eyes. Sunlight streamed through the window, and she could hear birds chirping outside. She started to roll over and bumped into something.

No, *someone.*

"Ow!" Piper said, beside her.

"What are you doing he—oh!" Last night came rushing back at her. They were in Prue's room. And this was the day they were leaving Montague House. "You guys, wake up. We have to get out of here."

"What time is it?" Piper mumbled.

"Past nine," Prue said, sitting up promptly and checking her travel alarm. "We've got some calls to make."

"Mmm." Phoebe burrowed under the sheet.

Her head throbbed and her stomach lurched. Five more minutes, she thought, closing her eyes again.

The last thing she wanted to do today was move even an inch. No, that wasn't exactly true. The last thing she wanted to do today was hang around Montague House. Something was definitely up with this place. The sooner they got out of here, the better. Just as soon as she'd had a few more minutes of sleep.

"Phoebe," Prue said, jabbing her arm. "Come on. We have to pack."

"I'm packed," Phoebe murmured.

"She never unpacked, remember?" Piper said, sitting up and stretching.

Prue swung her legs over the edge of the bed and reached for the phone on her bedside table. "I'll call around to some hotels while you two get ready."

"Mmm," Phoebe said, sitting up. She felt weak.

"Are you all right?" Prue asked. "You look really pale."

"I'm just tired," Phoebe said. "And my stomach still doesn't feel great."

"Just hang tight, Phoebs," Prue said. "As soon as we get settled somewhere, I'll find the number for the nearest doctor."

Phoebe groaned. "Last time I went to the doctor, he made me get a tetanus shot."

Piper was already heading for the hallway. "Better get dressed."

Phoebe sighed. She started to stand. "Whoa," she said, feeling dizzy. She sat down again and rubbed her temples. "This is not cool," she muttered, wanting desperately to lie down again.

Prue put her hand over the receiver. "Do you need help?" she asked in a worried voice.

"No, I can make it to my room," Phoebe insisted.

Phoebe stood up again, slowly this time. Clinging to the footboard for support, she took a few unsteady steps. So far so good.

She made her way down the wide hall to her room. The door was closed, but as she reached for the knob, a fleeting vision filled Phoebe's mind.

Another hand opening this door in the wee hours of the morning, when the hallway was still dark.

Someone searching her room, but for what—and what was the person's intent? The vision ended.

Phoebe hesitated before entering the room. What if somebody was lurking inside, waiting there to harm her?

But certain as she was that someone had been in her room, she was just as certain that that person had left before her return.

She opened the door slowly and peered inside. The room was empty, unless someone was hiding under the bed. She walked unsteadily over to the bed and yanked back the spread.

The space under the bed was empty.

Wearily, Phoebe sat on the bed. Her head was pounding like crazy. Maybe she could snatch just a few seconds of rest.

She was about to lower her head onto the pillow when she saw it.

"Prue! Piper!" she called.

Pounding footsteps sounded in the hall. A moment later her sisters burst into the room.

"What is it, Phoebe?" Prue asked, rushing over to her.

She pointed mutely at the symbol on the white pillowcase.

Prue gasped. "Where did that come from?"

Phoebe shook her head. She stared at the odd symbol that had been drawn there in what looked like black ink. It consisted of three interlocking stars inside a circle.

"It's a vèvè!" Piper exclaimed.

"Huh? What's a vèvè?" Phoebe asked.

"It's a symbol that represents a voodoo god," Prue explained. "We saw them at the voodoo museum yesterday."

"And I saw one at the ceremony last night," Piper said in a troubled voice. "Though it was a different design. This one must be for a different loa."

"Well, what's it doing in my bed?" Phoebe asked.

"I have no idea," Prue said slowly, staring at it. "But I don't think it's a good sign."

"This has gone too far. We have to get out of here," Phoebe said, backing away from the pillow.

"We *are* going," Prue said. "I haven't found a hotel yet, but I haven't given up hope. Let's pack our things, check out, and drive into New Orleans. We'll stop at the museum and talk to Gabrielle. Maybe she can recommend another place."

"Yeah. One without freaky rituals going on outside it," Phoebe put in.

"Fine with me," Piper said. "And while we're in the French Quarter, maybe we can check out Remy's one more time."

"Maybe," Prue said, throwing a worried glance Phoebe's way. "If we don't have a hotel by noon, we're going to the airport. Now let's pack."

It should have taken her all of two minutes to get her things together after her sisters left the room, but Phoebe found herself moving listlessly, feeling entirely drained of energy. Finally she zipped her duffel bag closed and shuffled out into the hall.

She went to Piper's room and found both her sisters in there. Prue's packed suitcase sat just inside the door. Piper's open bag was on the bed, and she was madly tossing things into it.

Phoebe set her own duffel beside Prue's bag and started across the room toward a chair. She had to sit down. If she didn't she felt as if she might actually fall.

The phone rang and Piper picked it up. "It's Gabrielle," she told her sisters. She listened for a moment, then said, "Actually, we were going to call you. We've decided to leave Montague House and we were wondering if you knew of any other hotels with openings."

She listened again, then put her palm over the receiver. "Gabrielle just invited us to stay with *her* for the rest of the week. She says she has a spare room in her flat, and there's plenty of room for all of us."

"We can't impose like that," Prue said at once.

Piper handed her the phone. "You tell her that."

Prue and Gabrielle talked for a few minutes, then Prue hung up. "I promised her we'd at least stop by the flat," she told her sisters.

"No, cher. It is not a good idea." A strange voice said from the doorway.

Phoebe turned and saw Yvonne standing in the doorway to Piper's room. She wore a blue dress. A blue madras scarf was tied over her head. Her eyes were focused on Piper's suitcase.

"What do you think you are doing?" Yvonne asked in her strange accent.

"We're leaving," Piper said. "We have to—"

"And going to stay where?" Yvonne demanded, coming into the room.

"I don't think that's any of your business," Prue said in a cool, challenging tone.

"You must not accept invitations to stay in

New Orleans." Yvonne narrowed her eyes, fastening her dark gaze on each of them in turn before saying, "You must leave the city at once."

"And if we don't?" Phoebe wanted to know.

"Then you will all die," the woman answered.

Phoebe's heart thudded in her chest. Yvonne was threatening them—threatening their lives!

Prue raised her arms abruptly. Yvonne flew up into the air and was pinned against the wall beside the door.

"We don't take kindly to threats," Prue warned in a low voice. "So don't mess with us. Got it?"

The older woman stared at them, speechless and trembling.

Phoebe peered into Yvonne's face. "You have no idea what kind of forces you're dealing with." She repeated the woman's own words back to her.

Prue lowered her arms.

Yvonne dropped to the floor. She quickly fled the room.

"See? I told you she was up to something," Phoebe said, turning to her sisters.

"You were right, Phoebe. I'm so sorry I didn't believe you all along." Prue grabbed her suitcase. "Come on. We are *so* out of here."

"First stop, the Toussaint Voodoo Museum," Prue announced to her sisters as they parked in front of the voodoo museum an hour later. After the run-in with Yvonne, they had pretty much blown right out of Montague House with their luggage.

Kane and Daphne had attempted to persuade them to stay longer, but Prue let them know in no uncertain terms that there would be no debate. She signed their bill and left.

"This is it?" Phoebe stared doubtfully at the building in front of them. "It doesn't look like a museum. It looks like a house."

"It definitely looks like a museum inside. You'll see," Prue said, blowing her damp hair back from her face as she led the way through the courtyard.

The midday sun beat down from the clear blue sky above. The air was still and soggy with humidity. The sisters stepped into the small entry hall. Prue walked behind Phoebe, watching her carefully. She seemed so weak from whatever bug she had. Prue hoped she'd feel better soon.

"That's strange," Prue murmured as she entered the building. The chair behind the desk was vacant, the electric fans motionless, the dozens of candles unlit.

"Maybe they're closed," Phoebe offered.

"Wouldn't the door be locked if they were?" Prue asked, taking a few tentative steps into the room.

"Somebody must be here," Piper said. "I just heard footsteps upstairs."

Prue cleared her throat and called, "Hello! Gabrielle? Helene?"

"Who's there?" a voice called down.

"It's Prue Halliwell," she answered, relieved. "Is that you, Gabrielle?"

"Yes." Hurried footsteps pounded down the steps, and Gabrielle Toussaint appeared in the room.

Today she was wearing modern clothing: a yellow polo shirt, khaki shorts, and sandals. Her hair was loose and wavy around her face. There was a troubled expression in her blue eyes.

"What's wrong, Gabrielle?" Prue asked.

"It's Helene. She never came home last night."

"Is that unusual?" Prue asked.

"For Helene it is. She is always here in the morning. When I called you this morning, she was a little late, but I was sure she'd walk in at any moment. But she never did."

"How do you know she never went home last night?" Piper asked.

"Because I had left her several messages that she didn't return," Gabrielle said.

"Maybe she didn't want to call you back," Phoebe said with a smirk. "I mean, I know that when my older sisters are checking up on me, sometimes I resent it."

"No, she always calls me when she gets in, to let me know she's home safely. And when I called her apartment this morning, there was a long, long beep on the answering machine, which means she never played her messages last night."

"She was probably out, having a good time,"

Phoebe suggested. "Maybe when she got home, she was so tired she forgot about her messages."

"No, not Helene. She's not a party girl. And she always plays her messages. Look, I know that something is wrong. I know this has something to do with one of the secret sociétés. She's been . . . involved with them before. That's why I was in such a hurry to get home from San Francisco. Fortunately, while I was away, Andre was looking out for her. He found her on the way to a ceremony and convinced her not to go. I was hoping that would be the end of it."

Prue's stomach turned over. She remembered the conversation she'd overheard between Andre and Gabrielle, and she knew how she'd feel if one of her sisters were in that kind of danger. "Is there anything we can do to help, Gabrielle?"

"Thank you, but I can't think of anything. Andre is out searching for her now. I've been turning tourists away all morning. I keep thinking maybe he'll call and say he's found her, but . . ."

"I'm sure she'll turn up sometime soon," Piper said comfortingly.

"I hope so," Gabrielle said. "What she's involved in may be very dangerous. It makes me feel so powerless," she added in a small voice. "And alone." Gabrielle walked over to the window.

Prue glanced at her sisters. She knew they felt the same way she did. Not one of them could imagine what it would be like to lose a sister. They'd each be devastated—heartbroken. And they'd need all the support they could get.

"Well, what do you think?" Prue spoke up.

"We can't abandon Gabrielle," Piper said. "She needs us." She huddled closer to Prue and Phoebe. "And we're out of the Montague House— why not hang out with Gabrielle until Helene turns up?"

Phoebe sighed. "As long as I can stay as immobile as possible, it's fine with me."

"Gabrielle, if you'd like, my sisters and I will stay with you," Prue offered. "Maybe we can help you cope until Helene returns."

"Really?" Gabrielle turned from the window. Her expression brightened. "That would be just . . . that would be so kind of you."

"No problem," Piper said, putting an arm around her.

"Why don't you put a Closed sign on the door?" Prue suggested. "That way, you won't have to deal with tourists popping in."

Gabrielle nodded reluctantly. "I hate to lose a day's business—we're still trying to get the museum off the ground. But right now all that matters is finding Helene."

She walked over to the door, flipped the Closed sign in the window, and turned to the Halliwells as she opened the door. "Let's go to Helene's apartment," she said. "It's not far from here, and I have a key. We can wait there."

Prue, Piper, and Phoebe stepped out into the muggy afternoon and waited while Gabrielle locked up the museum. Then they set off down a narrow street. Prue noticed that the French Quarter that had seemed so colorfully quaint now seemed almost garish. The colorful street characters, the honky-tonk music blasting from speakers . . .

Suddenly all she wanted was to get on a plane and flee with her sisters back to San Francisco. But they couldn't. Not until they were sure Gabrielle's sister was all right.

Phoebe clutched the railing as she climbed the steps to Helene's apartment, aware that the others were moving more swiftly, several steps above her. The apartment was in an old three-story apartment building, and the stairs were steep, the treads uneven.

She felt weak, wanting to sink down on a step to rest, but she forced herself to keep climbing. Now wasn't the time to worry Prue and Piper. Not when Gabrielle was so distraught over her own sister's disappearance.

"Are you all right?" Piper asked, turning to look at Phoebe from the top of the stairs as Prue and Gabrielle disappeared around a corner.

"I'm fine," Phoebe said, trying to catch her breath. "It's just so darned hot."

At least that was true, she thought, wiping a trickle of sweat from the back of her neck. It had to be a hundred degrees out in the sun, and even warmer in this stuffy old building.

Piper looked carefully at her for a long moment, then nodded. "It is hot," she agreed. "Maybe you're dehydrated. You look awfully weak."

"I'll be fine when I get a glass of water," Phoebe insisted, reaching the top of the stairs.

She and Piper caught up with Prue and Gabrielle down a narrow, windowless corridor that was lined with three closed doors and lit only by a bare, dim-watted bulb high overhead.

Gabrielle had stopped at the last door and was fumbling with a key in the lock. Moments later she got it unlatched and threw open the door. She stepped inside, followed by Prue and Piper. Phoebe walked through the doorway last, just as she heard Gabrielle cry out.

"What is it?" Phoebe asked, rushing forward.

She found herself in a small, shabbily furnished room. Several chairs were overturned, the worn area rug was rumpled, and the pictures on the wall were askew. A tall black floor fan had toppled over, and several potted plants had been knocked from a small stand by the window, scattering dirt all over the carpet.

"Something's happened," Gabrielle said, wide-eyed as she looked around at the mess. "Someone was in here." Her voice rose with panic. "Helene must have fought them!"

Phoebe stood paralyzed. There *was* something sinister here. She could feel it. She felt herself wobbling and held on to the door frame for support.

"I'm afraid to go into the bedroom," Gabrielle was saying, clutching Prue's arm. "What if . . . what if we find her here? What if she's . . . ?"

"If she's here, she needs our help," Prue told her gently. "It's all right. We're with you, Gabrielle."

Phoebe stumbled a few steps, making her way into the apartment. She sank into a nearby sofa as her sisters and Gabrielle walked slowly toward the next room.

She picked up a throw pillow and hugged it to her chest. As she did, she inhaled an unfamiliar floral scent. Perfume.

A vision suddenly lit her mind, coming brilliantly to life, like a rural evening landscape beneath a flash of lightning.

A brown-eyed beauty she'd never seen before appeared before her. Phoebe knew instinctively that she was Gabrielle's sister Helene—and that she was in danger.

Her vision expanded, and she could see that the girl was standing in the middle of a circle, surrounded by red-robed figures. They were chanting something. Drums were beating in a peculiar, irregular rhythm.

The girl's body convulsed.

She began to quake violently.

Her skin grew pallid.

Her eyes rolled back into her head.

"Phoebe!"

She started, and the vision disappeared.

She saw Piper standing over her. "What are you doing?"

"I'm just . . . I saw something," she said, just as Gabrielle cried out from the next room.

Piper grabbed Phoebe's arm and pulled her into the small bedroom.

On the mirror above the dresser was a strange, intricate symbol drawn in scarlet. There were a series of interlocking triangles and swirling lines surrounded by a circle.

"Is it blood?" Gabrielle asked fearfully.

"It's lipstick," Prue said, leaning closer. "It's a vèvè, isn't it?"

Gabrielle nodded. "It's the symbol for one of the Petro loas, Zdenek."

"A Petro loa is one of the bad ones, right?" Phoebe asked in a low voice.

Prue nodded, stroking Gabrielle's hair in an effort to calm her trembling.

"Zdenek's rituals involve human sacrifice," Gabrielle told the Halliwells.

"But where did it come from?" Piper asked.

"The secret société must have left it when they took Helene." Gabrielle convulsed into sobs.

"Shh," Prue comforted. "We'll find her, Gabrielle."

"I have to tell Andre," Gabrielle said suddenly. "I've got to call him."

"I thought he was out looking for her," Piper said.

"He is, but I'll leave him a message. He needs to know what we're dealing with. The phone is in the kitchen. I'll be right back."

She left the room.

"I had a vision of Helene," Phoebe said hurriedly to her sisters. "She's in serious trouble. I saw her in some kind of ceremony, and I sensed that her life was in danger."

"Phoebe's right," Piper said grimly, gesturing at the mirror. "Did you hear what Gabrielle said about that loa, Zdenek?"

Prue and Phoebe nodded slowly.

Phoebe took a deep breath. "Guys, when we discovered our powers, we promised to use them to fight evil and to help people in danger," she said in a whisper. "If Helene's situation doesn't qualify under both counts, I don't know what does."

"You're right, Phoebe," Prue nodded. "We have to help Gabrielle."

"But, Phoebe, can you help?" Piper asked. "I mean, you are looking really sick. We should probably get you to a doctor."

"No way," Phoebe said stubbornly. So what if her head ached and her stomach was queasy and she couldn't seem to get past this dizziness? "If you two stay, I stay. You might need the Power of Three."

Her sisters nodded slowly.

"If you're sure you're okay, Phoebe," Piper told her, squeezing her shoulders.

"Don't worry about me. I'll be fine," Phoebe said with a lot more confidence than she actually felt.

CHAPTER
8

I think we should call a doctor," Prue said a few hours later, watching Phoebe shiver beneath a quilt on Gabrielle's couch. She didn't like her sister's pale face or the way her voice sounded—all weak and far away, as though it was a major effort just for her to talk.

"Definitely," Piper said, beside her.

Phoebe shook her head. "Guys, I'll be fine. All I need is to catch up on some rest. By tomorrow I'll be back to normal. You'll see."

Prue hesitated, then shrugged. "Okay, we'll see, but if you're not better by tomorrow morning, we're calling a doctor."

She was tired herself, she realized. It had grown dark outside the windows. She sank heavily into an antique green-upholstered chair beside the couch.

Gabrielle's apartment was small, but she'd decorated it with flair. The spare room that Prue and her sisters were sharing was surprisingly airy, with a deep closet that, fortunately, held all their luggage. The flat was on the ground floor of an old house on the fringes of the French Quarter. The street was quiet, almost an alleyway, totally off the beaten path. The three rooms had uneven floorboards and low-beamed ceilings and were furnished with great, shabby-chic pieces—overstuffed velvet chairs, a worn Oriental carpet, old brass lamps with fringed silk shades. The only clue that this was the twenty-first century was the large air-conditioning unit that hummed in the living room window, cooling the entire apartment.

Gabrielle had told the sisters to make themselves at home while she went out to get some groceries from the market down the street. "I don't have a thing to eat in the house," she'd said apologetically. "And when I'm worried, I get hungry."

Prue and her sisters had begged her not to go to any trouble. But she had insisted she needed the distraction to take her mind off Helene, because she was going crazy with worry.

"What do you think that is?" Piper asked, pointing to a small rectangular table in the corner of the living room. It was draped with a black cloth; on it were several candles and a shallow basket filled with what looked like bunches of dried herbs.

"Gabrielle said she practices voodoo," Prue reminded her, noting that Phoebe's eyes had closed. She seemed to have dozed off. "It looks like some kind of altar."

"Well, it gives me the creeps," Piper said with a shudder.

"It shouldn't. Gabrielle said her rituals involve the positive forces, remember? The Rada loa, not the Petro loa."

"Still . . ."

"Come on, Piper, how do you think she'd feel if she knew about us?" Prue pointed out.

Piper shrugged. "Let's just hope she never finds out. I'm still not crazy about the fact that Yvonne saw what you can do."

"I know, but . . ." Prue shook her head, remembering the dangerous gleam in the old woman's eyes. "I couldn't let her threaten us. I figured if she had a taste of what she was up against, she'd back off."

"But what if we've only made her angrier?" Piper asked. "What if she—"

"Shh," Prue cautioned, hearing a key in the lock. "Gabrielle's back."

"Oh, let me help," Piper said, hurrying toward Gabrielle, who was struggling to balance two large paper bags full of groceries in one arm. She had almost reached her when something loomed up in the shadows behind Gabrielle.

"Look out!" Prue shrieked.

A jolt went through her as she glimpsed the

figure's unnaturally pale face. The eyes rolled up into its head.

Oh my God! Prue thought. It's Helene!

The girl's beautiful features had been changed, disfigured somehow.

Gabrielle ducked, and Helene's hands closed around Piper's throat, jerking her backward. Piper made a strangled sound, struggling blindly against the ferocious assault, her hands clawing at the air.

"Do something, Prue!" Phoebe shrieked, bolting from the couch behind them.

Prue rushed forward, past Gabrielle who now cowered against the wall. She grabbed hold of Helene's arms and struggled with her, screaming, "Piper, get away! Now!"

Piper managed to slip from Helene's grasp. Prue felt ice-cold hands lock around her own throat. She struggled futilely to pry them apart, but Helene was far stronger than she'd guessed. Inhumanly strong. From the corner of her eye, Prue saw Piper's arms fly up.

Abruptly time stood still.

"Hurry, Prue," Piper said frantically, "before it wears off."

Prue pried Helene's deathlike grip from her neck and spun around. Her heart sank as she felt a minute shift in the air—the time freeze was already beginning to wear off. Helene was beginning to move. Without thinking, Prue used her powers to knock her off her feet. Helene was hurled backward, landing outside the door.

Piper rushed forward to slam and lock the door before Helene could get up.

Gabrielle blinked, looking stunned. "What happened? Where's Helene?"

As if in answer, Helene slammed her weight against the other side of the door, pounding on the old, splintered wood, and then began crying out with long, anguished howls. Prue felt chills race down her spine. The sound was eerie, more animal than human.

"Helene?" Gabrielle started toward the door.

"No!" Prue intercepted Gabrielle, pulling her into her arms. "Helene's . . . not herself," she told Gabrielle in as calm a voice as she could muster. "You can't open the door now. She's dangerous."

Gabrielle squirmed in Prue's grasp, straining toward the door. "She's my sister!" she sobbed.

Prue struggled to hold Gabrielle back. "Piper, Phoebe, a little help here!"

They tumbled to the floor. Her sisters managed to get hold of Gabrielle's flailing arms, pinning her down as Helene screeched outside, banging on the door and windows.

"You can't help her now!" Prue told a wild-eyed Gabrielle. "Can't you see? She wants to hurt you!"

"Oh, Helene," Gabrielle wailed, growing limp beneath their grasp. "How did this happen? How could they have done this to you?"

"What is it?" Piper asked. "What's the matter with her?"

Tears were pouring down Gabrielle's cheeks. "The secret société," she sobbed. "They did this to her. She is lost now. I will never have my sister back again."

Prue tried to keep her own voice steady. "Gabrielle, I need you to calm down," she said. "What do you mean, she's lost now? What did they do to her?"

"The société," Gabrielle answered. "They turned her into a zombie."

"A zombie?" Prue echoed, glancing from Gabrielle's tortured face to the shocked expressions in her sisters' eyes.

They all knew what a zombie was.

The living dead. A walking corpse.

But that was something out of horror films. Not a real being, pounding on the other side of the door.

Gabrielle continued to sob, at first hysterical, then growing more subdued as the terrifying pounding continued for what seemed like an eternity.

Finally all grew quiet.

"She's gone," Gabrielle wept softly. "My poor sister. My poor sister."

Phoebe frowned in her seat on the couch. "How could this happen?" she asked. "Excuse me if this isn't exactly a tactful question, but how could the société turn Helene into a zombie?"

"They fed her a very powerful toxin," Gabrielle

answered in a flat tone. "When someone is poisoned like that, the person appears to be dead. So, usually, they are buried. But the voodoo practitioner who poisoned the victim, unearths the body and then 'revives' it, using other herbs and spells. The victim is in a kind of suspended comatose state, capable only of obeying the one who has poisoned her. She has no will of her own, no life spirit. She is no longer the person she was. She is an automaton, a slave. Her body will be used by its new master for a short time—until it dies."

"So there's no cure?" Phoebe asked.

"None that I have ever heard of," Gabrielle replied. "To make a zombie requires very powerful magic and the summoning of very powerful spirits. It is not something that can just be undone."

Prue stroked Gabrielle's dark hair, knowing there was nothing she could possibly say to make this better.

"What are we going to do now?" Piper asked in a low voice. She glanced nervously at the door. "I mean, what if she's still out there? Hiding or something?"

Prue got to her feet.

"Prue, you're not going out there?" Phoebe asked anxiously.

"No," she told her sister.

She crossed slowly to the door and parted the old-fashioned lace curtains that covered the window beside it. Peering out, she saw no sign of Helene.

She crossed to the window facing the street and did the same. No Helene there either. But in the glow from the lamppost by the step, she could see something else. Something hanging from an azalea bush to the left of the door.

It appeared to be a scrap of fabric.

She gasped, recognizing the blue madras pattern of the scarf Yvonne had been wearing that morning. Had the old woman been here too? Had she followed the Charmed Ones to Gabrielle's? Had she seen Helene show up?

Or did she have something to do with Helene's being turned into a zombie? Could *she* have done it herself? Was she the one who now controlled Helene?

The only thing Prue knew for certain was that she and her sisters might be out of the Montague House, but they weren't safe yet. Not by a long shot.

"Why are we going back to this con woman again?" Prue asked Piper as the two of them hurried along the bustling, well-lit street. Revelers spilled out of bars wearing strings of brightly colored beads. A Dixieland band on the corner played a jaunty tune that hardly reflected Prue's mood.

"Because she obviously knows a lot about voodoo," Piper answered. "If Gabrielle doesn't know how to help Helene—"

"And she doesn't," Prue put in.

"Madame La Roux might be our only option—and our only hope."

"What makes you think this place is even going to be open at this hour?"

"Because check it out, Prue. Does it look like anything in this town ever closes?" Piper answered dryly.

Jazz, ragtime, blues, and Cajun music spilled out into the street from the variety of clubs and restaurants that lined the block. The coffee bars wafted their fragrant aroma of freshly ground beans into the sultry summer night. Shops were brightly lit, offering everything from pralines to T-shirts to souvenir salt shakers.

"I guess you're right," Prue said. She pointed toward Madame La Roux's well-lit market stall. "Look, there it is."

"Do you think Phoebe will be okay?" Piper asked just before they stepped inside. "She's not looking any better than she did this morning."

"She's with Gabrielle," Prue said. "Gabrielle promised she'd keep an eye on her. And we won't be gone long."

The little shop was empty, except for the flame-haired proprietress, who looked up sharply when they walked in.

"You're back," she said.

"I wasn't sure you'd remember us," Prue told her. "You must have hundreds of tourists in here every day."

"Not all of them are foolish enough to be staying at the Montague House," Madame La Roux said with a shrug. "You, I remember. You were cursed the moment you crossed over the threshold of that house, and the curse will follow you wherever you go—unless you remove it." She reached underneath the counter. "I just happen to have a special powder here that can—"

"Hang on a minute, Madame," Prue cut in. "We're not dealing with a curse here. We're dealing with a big, bad, voodoo-wielding cook who turns people into zombies." Madame La Roux gasped and glanced up sharply.

That got her attention, Prue thought. "Now, how do we stop her?"

"I could tell you . . . if you were willing to dabble in black magic," the woman said ominously.

Prue looked at Piper. "It makes sense," she said after a moment, "that we'd have to fight voodoo with voodoo."

"Yeah, but black magic?" Piper asked doubtfully. "I don't want to have anything to do with that."

"There is another way," Madame La Roux said. She reached beneath the counter again. This time she pulled out a small white envelope and a yellowed sheet of paper. "This packet contains a powder that must be sprinkled on the ground around you if you are threatened in any way. As you sprinkle it, you must read the incantation printed on this paper."

"Is that going to help us with a zombie?" Prue demanded.

"It will protect you from all dangers," the red-haired woman assured her. "It is powerful."

Prue reached for the packet and the incantation, but the woman held them up, out of her reach.

"Ah-ah-ah," she said, wagging a finger at the sisters. "First you pay. And I'm warning you, this doesn't come cheaply."

She named a figure.

"Jeez, what's in there? Solid gold nuggets?" Prue asked. She looked at Piper, who nodded. They had no choice; they were going to need whatever protection they could get. Prue reached into her pocket for her credit card.

Madame La Roux's bracelets jangled as she reached out and snatched it. Prue held out her hand, and the woman dropped the packet and the spell onto her palm.

"Don't worry," Madame La Roux said as she swiped the credit card through her machine. "That will keep you safe."

Prue frowned. Maybe it would. Maybe it wouldn't. All she could hope for was that the powder and incantation—combined with the Power of Three—would buy them some time while they figured out just what Yvonne was up to . . . and how to stop her.

"So are you going to go to the police?" Piper asked Gabrielle. She and Prue had just returned from their visit to Madame La Roux. Now that they had the protective powder, what they needed was a plan of action.

"What good would it do?" Gabrielle replied. She was curled up in the green velvet chair, hugging her arms around herself as if she was cold. "The police don't want to know about voodoo. Besides, there's nothing anyone can do once someone has been turned into a zombie."

"Maybe," Prue agreed. "But I can't believe we should just give up on Helene. Besides, maybe the police can stop the secret société before they zombie-ize someone else."

Gabrielle shrugged listlessly and stared at the worn carpet.

"Gabrielle?" Piper prodded.

"Believe me, the police are helpless against voodoo," the young woman said. "It's like sending a rabbit to fight a tiger." She gave a defeated shrug. "But maybe I should go talk to them. I suppose it can't hurt to try."

"Okay," Piper said. She glanced at her sisters. "Now, what about us?"

Phoebe scrunched her eyes shut. "I hate to say it, but I think we have to go back to the bayou."

"Why?" Gabrielle sounded alarmed.

"Because that's where we saw the Petro loa cult," Piper answered. "They hold ceremonies every night. I'm not sure that particular group has anything to do with what's happened to Helene, but Prue is pretty sure Yvonne was in your alley when Helene attacked—so there's a chance that there's a connection between the cult behind the Montague House and Helene."

"It's the only lead we've got," Prue put in. "It's the only way to find out what's really going on."

Gabrielle's eyes went wide with fear. "It would be terribly dangerous for you to go back there."

Piper held up the little packet of white powder. "No worry," she said much more confidently than she felt. "We've got protection." She glanced at Phoebe, whose skin was a sickly shade of green. "But maybe you should stay here with Gabrielle," she added. "You don't look like you're up for a trip."

Piper knew that Phoebe didn't want them to go hunting a voodoo cult without the Power of Three. Still, she wasn't sure that taking Phoebe along was a good idea. How much power could Phoebe give them when she barely seemed capable of standing upright?

"Tell you what, Phoebe," Prue said. "Why don't you stay here with Gabrielle, and if we need you, we'll come back for you. I promise."

"No," Phoebe said simply. "I'm coming with you. End of discussion."

"I wish I had stayed back in the city with Gabrielle," Phoebe said in a small voice. She followed her sisters along the dark path leading into the misty depths of the bayou behind the Montague House.

"We told you to stay," Prue reminded her. "You wanted to come."

"Because I felt a little better after I rested," Phoebe lied. In truth, she hadn't rested at all while her sisters had been visiting Madame La Roux. She had done her best to fall asleep as Gabrielle sat in a chair by the window, grieving. But, exhausted as she had been, sleep wouldn't come. She couldn't seem to shake the overwhelming feeling of uneasiness that only grew stronger as the night wore on into the wee hours.

Now, after a silent car trip out into the bayou country, past the deserted town of Gaspard, she had to fight back the edge of panic that rose in her throat. Prue had parked the car under cover of the dense undergrowth along the road leading to the plantation, and the big old house had appeared dark and deserted as they skirted along the edge of the property.

Still, Phoebe couldn't help feeling that something horrible was going to happen at any moment. The Montague House—with Yvonne and her black magic—scared her. There was no doubt about it.

She reminded herself that at least they were armed with Madame La Roux's magical powder and spell. Not that the thought gave her much comfort. But when push came to shove, as lousy as she felt, and no matter how afraid she was, there was no way Phoebe could abandon her sisters at a time like this.

Get a grip, Phoebe, she coached herself. You're a
Charmed One. Everything's going to be fine. She
picked her way along a path that seemed to grow
darker and more menacing with every step. Prue
carried a flashlight borrowed from Gabrielle, but
even its bright beam, held low on the path in front
of them, seemed to do little to dispel the oppressive
darkness of the night.

All around them were the noises of the swamp—
the calling of night birds, the hum of insects, the
splashing and rustling as nocturnal animals stirred.
Above them rose the moss-draped trees, stretching
up into the clouds of mist that hung low in the dark,
moonless sky. The air was humid and heavily laced
with the smell of dank water and wet earth. The
ground beneath Phoebe's feet was spongy in some
spots, wet with mud in others.

I don't want to meet up with any snakes
tonight, she silently prayed. And no alligators
either!

"Some vacation," Piper muttered in a low
voice.

"Shh," Prue said, ahead of them.

"I'd rather be at Remy's," Piper whispered to
Phoebe. "How about you? Bet you'd rather be at
Seven Tuesdays, dancing the night away."

Phoebe shrugged. Under normal circum-
stances, she definitely would rather have been
out on the town. But she felt awful and was getting worse by the second. All she wanted was for
this whole nightmare to be over so she could

crawl into her own bed and sleep for, like, a week.

Prue stopped short on the path ahead and motioned for Phoebe and Piper to creep forward.

"It's the secret société," Piper confirmed, nodding.

Phoebe heard voices nearby, murmuring something that sounded like a prayer—or a chant.

Prue parted the branches of a low-hanging tree and held a finger to her lips as she looked at her sisters, then ahead into the clearing.

Phoebe followed her gaze.

It was all she could do not to gasp at the macabre scene before them.

A circle of masked, red-robed figures stood beneath a tall canopy of thatched wood. A flickering fire roared in the center. The figures' arms were raised to the sky, heads bent backward as they chanted words in a language Phoebe had never heard before. One of the taller figures held a headless chicken over a brass bowl, laughing as its blood poured out.

Phoebe grimaced. She felt a sour liquid rise in the back of her throat.

As the sisters watched, one of the figures began to beat a drum. It began slowly, quietly, an irregular rhythm that picked up its pace as the chanting grew louder and higher-pitched.

Phoebe's heart began to pound. She didn't like this at all. They had to get out of here. *Now.* Before it was too late.

"Prue! Piper!" She reached out to touch her sisters' hands.

Prue and Piper turned to look at her.

"Please," Phoebe said, her voice barely audible. She paused, swallowed hard against another rush of bile in her throat. Then, fighting for strength, she whispered, "Something terrible is happening."

Phoebe felt as though the drumbeats and the voices were alive—actual beings closing in on her. She opened her mouth, trying to breathe in air, knowing she had to calm herself. But it was as though she were being smothered slowly by the many spirits descending on her.

Frantic, no longer able to speak, she silently begged her sisters for help. She reached out for Prue's arm.

Didn't they feel it? Couldn't they sense what was happening here? Weren't they aware of the evil forces that swirled in the night air around them?

"Piper, something's wrong with Phoebe. Give me the incantation, the powder," Prue said urgently, holding out her hand. Her worried eyes now stared at Phoebe. Phoebe could just make out Prue's face as the world began to spin before her.

She heard her sisters hurriedly murmuring the words printed on a sheet of paper they held in the flashlight's beam, then saw Prue open a small white packet and quickly sprinkle the contents around them.

The drumbeats grew louder.

The chanting more persistent.

Phoebe stretched her arms toward her sisters. The protection wasn't working.

Please! her own voice shrieked inside of her head. Please don't let them take me!

But her sisters suddenly seemed very far away; their voices fading into the roar that suddenly filled Phoebe's ears.

Prue, Piper . . . please . . .

Can't you see what's happening?

All at once, everything went black.

CHAPTER
9

What's happening?" Piper questioned. A bank of fog came out of nowhere and closed over her, blinding her. She tried to grab for Phoebe, who'd been standing inches away, but her hands felt only empty space. She saw only a veil of whirling white.

"Prue!" Piper cried out.

"I'm here!" Prue yelled back. "Phoebe? Phoebe!" Piper heard her sister cry.

There was no reply. The drumbeats and chants reached a crescendo, and then . . . silence.

The mist was thicker now, almost solid. Piper stretched out her hand, hoping to touch either one of her sisters. They'd been here seconds ago. They couldn't be more than a few inches away. But all she could feel was a thick, clammy dampness.

Then the mist lifted as suddenly as it had descended. Piper could see again.

Prue stood directly opposite her. But what about Phoebe? Where was she? Piper whirled around in disbelief.

Phoebe was gone.

The secret société was gone. There was nothing beneath the canopy except the smoldering fire and a splattering of blood on the ground.

"Phoebe!" Prue yelled. "Phoebe!"

"Where is she, Prue?" Piper asked, her voice wavering. "Where is she?"

"I don't know." Prue stalked toward the site of the voodoo ceremony. "Phoebe!"

Piper wanted to collapse, to just crumple onto the ground and give up, right there. But she couldn't. She had to keep her wits about her, for Phoebe's sake. "We have to find her," she choked out.

"We will," Prue said, but her usual cool, in-control manner was gone. Her voice was shaking. She snapped her head around to gaze directly at Piper. "Hey! What was that spell we used to find Phoebe the time she took off with that motorcycle freak she met over in North Beach?"

Piper's heart lifted. Yes! That incantation *had* worked. It was sure to point the way to Phoebe. She remembered how, last time they had used this particular spell, Phoebe had instantly popped up in the attic wearing a motorcycle helmet and a black leather jacket. She was royally pissed at her sisters for interrupting her "date."

"Great idea! I'm sure I can remember the spell," Piper said. "Quick, hold my hands." With their fingers interlocked, Piper chanted, "Search north and south and east and west for one who's left our humble nest. Search land and sea and sky above; bring safely back the one we love."

There was a rush of wind, a force so powerful that it swept them both into the air and spun them around. It vanished abruptly, setting them on their feet again, both facing in the same direction.

Piper opened her eyes and looked around. "No Phoebe," she said dejectedly.

"No," Prue agreed. "Looks like this time all the spell gave us is a direction."

"Which is?"

Prue looked up at the sky, then said, "Southeast. Toward New Orleans."

"I don't suppose you have a spell for narrowing that down a little?" Piper asked.

"Nope. Come on, we'd better get going."

"But we don't even know where in the city we're supposed to start," Piper protested.

"Which is why we'd better not waste time," Prue pointed out. "She could be anywhere. And who knows how long she has before . . ."

"Before . . ." Piper echoed, her eyes meeting her sister's. She didn't like the look she saw there. She tore her gaze away. "Yeah," she muttered. "We'd better not waste time."

*   *   *

After parking the rental car, Prue and Piper walked along Bourbon Street, discussing where to start. The spell hadn't merely given them a direction. It was still working. Prue could feel it pulling at her, drawing her like a magnet through the narrow streets of the French Quarter—toward Phoebe. She was somewhere in this section of the city, Prue thought. She had to be. She glanced at building after building, wondering if each one might be headquarters for the secret société. But the spell continued to draw them on.

They passed a small park. Prue shivered. She could have sworn she felt a pair of eyes on her, watching her from the shadowy trees just beyond the sidewalk. She turned around.

"What's the matter?" Piper asked.

"Nothing," she said. No one was near. No one who appeared to be following them, anyway.

"Should we call Gabrielle?" Piper asked as they passed a pay phone. "She'll be waiting for us, wanting to know what we found out. And maybe she's heard from Phoebe."

"We might as well." Prue fished in her pocket for some change and put it into the slot. She dialed, then waited as the phone rang and rang. Finally she hung up and turned to Piper. "No one's there."

"She's probably doing what we're doing," Piper said. "Combing the streets for Helene or someone who can help her."

As Prue turned away from the phone, the pull

of the spell intensified, turning her body toward the other side of the street. A sign there caught her eye. "Piper, look!" she exclaimed, pointing.

Piper turned around and gasped. "It's the club where Helene's boyfriend, Andre, works."

Prue nodded, staring at the flashing neon sign that read, Seven Tuesdays: All Mardi Gras, All The Time. Even from the crowded, noisy street they could hear the throbbing music emanating from the two-story nightclub.

"It's no coincidence that we're here," Prue said, feeling a glimmer of hope. "The spell's been pulling us all along. That club is where we're supposed to go. Phoebe's got to be close by."

"Then let's go in," Piper said.

They made their way past the noisy, wild crowd drinking in the street in front of the club. Many of the revelers wore masks, and some had on giant papier-mâché heads. Somebody wearing a dragon head put several strings of beads around Prue's neck as she passed by, and somebody else spilled a drink on her legs.

Prue focused on the open door of the nightclub, letting the spell pull her inside. The hair prickled on the back of her neck as she stepped over the threshold into the deafening, jampacked room.

Was it even remotely possible that they'd find Phoebe here?

And even if she was here, how would they possibly spot her?

Everywhere Prue looked she saw people dressed in sequined masks and strange costumes. Strobe lights flashed over a dance floor that jammed with bodies, and the bar was packed ten deep. The air was heavy with the scent of cigarette smoke and beer.

"Prue, look," Piper shouted above the noise.

She saw that her sister was pointing in the direction of the bar. Frowning, she wondered what Piper meant.

And then she saw him—Andre.

She'd known he worked here, but somehow she hadn't really expected to find him at his job after all that had happened with Helene. She narrowed her eyes, watching him as he expertly uncapped a couple of beer bottles.

Get a grip, Prue, what's he supposed to do— sob at the bar? she scolded herself. He was just doing his job. Anyone looking at Prue and Piper might not realize they were living their worst nightmare either.

"Let's go talk to him," Piper yelled.

Prue nodded. They started moving toward the bar. Along the way a group of drunken frat boys put a beer into each of their hands, whooping and hollering.

Prue looked at Piper, who shrugged.

"To Phoebe," she said over the noise, clinking her bottle against Prue's.

"To Phoebe." Prue took a sip.

She and Piper continued to make their way

toward the bar, but it was like trying to swim upstream against a major current. For every two steps they managed to edge forward, they found themselves forced to take a step back.

Prue looked up at one point and found that they were standing near a sign that read Rest Rooms. Was it even remotely possible that Phoebe might be in the ladies' room? she asked herself. Well, if she was, it wouldn't be any weirder than anything else that had happened so far. And since they were here now, they might as well check. Prue tugged on Piper's sleeve. "I'm going into the bathroom," she yelled, fighting to be heard above the music.

"What?" Piper raised her hands to show that she hadn't heard.

Prue gestured at the sign above her head.

Piper, understanding, nodded and motioned that she'd be waiting right outside the door.

Prue pushed open the wooden door and found herself in a long, dark hallway. She made her way down it, passing clusters of masked club-goers who seemed to turn and stare menacingly after her. She began to feel woozy, as though the walls were closing in on her. What's wrong with me? she wondered.

Air. She needed air, that was all. She had to get out of this hallway.

She hesitated, turning back toward the door to the club. Was it her distorted perception, or had the figures in the hallway formed a human blockade in front of it?

She spun around. In front of her stood three doors bearing signs that read Ladies, Gentlemen, and Exit. She burst through the last door, and found herself in a narrow, dingy alleyway. Prue took in great gulping breaths anyway, leaning against the brick wall of the club. Nothing here but a few parked cars, a towering stack of wooden crates, and a large trash Dumpster. The stench of garbage hung in the air.

Prue turned to go back into the door, then froze as she saw something move in the shadows beyond the Dumpster.

"Who's there?" she called.

There was a shuffling sound on the pavement.

"Who's there?" she asked again.

No answer—just an ominous silence.

Panic rose in Prue's throat. She reached blindly behind her, her back pressed against the wall, her hand fumbling for the knob of the door. Her fingers closed around it.

She turned and tugged at it with all her might, but it wouldn't budge. It had locked behind her.

She felt the presence behind her even before she saw the long shadow cast on the brick wall. Her breath caught as she turned slowly and found herself face-to-face with the zombie— Helene Toussaint.

The girl's expressionless face was inches from her own. Her vacant eyes were fastened on Prue; her arms outstretched, reaching . . .

"No!" Prue screamed. She whirled around,

searching desperately for an escape. There was
none. Her only hope was to use her powers to
hurl Helene against the wall.

But when she raised her arms, nothing happened.

My God, I must have been drugged, she
thought wildly. Somebody put something in that
beer. But who? There was no time to figure it out.
Helene's icy hands fastened around Prue's
throat.

Prue wrenched herself free from the viselike
grip, managing to knock the zombie to the
ground. But Helene couldn't be stopped. Her
arms closed around Prue's leg and pulled, bringing her down.

"Ow!" Prue hit the ground hard, then twisted
frantically, struggling to get away.

As she fought off Helene's powerful grip, she
became aware of someone standing above them.
She glanced up. Her breath caught in her throat
when she recognized the silhouette.

"Phoebe!" she said in a strangled voice as
Helene grabbed her in a headlock. "Phoebe,
help!"

Helene was pressing against her windpipe
now, choking off her air supply. Prue raised her
knee and jabbed it as hard as she could into
Helene's stomach, forcing her to loosen her grasp
momentarily.

Prue took advantage, scrambling to her feet.
"Come on, Phoebe, let's go!" she shouted.

But Phoebe just stood there, her face a grotesque mask devoid of expression.

What's happened to her? Prue wondered.

Phoebe's eyes rolled up into her head. Prue felt her body go numb with shock and horror as the realization hit. . . .

Phoebe was a zombie!

CHAPTER
10

Phoebe, for God's sake, help me!" Prue shrieked.

Helene stood. She moved toward Prue with a stiff, robotic walk that made Prue's blood run cold. The girl wasn't human anymore. She was barely alive.

Prue eyed the stack of crates that towered above Helene. All she had to do was give them a shove, and the heavy wooden boxes would come tumbling down on top of the zombie.

But Phoebe was there, her eyes horribly blank. She would be crushed by the falling boxes, too.

Phoebe moved toward her, with that same awful walk, shoulder-to-shoulder with Helene.

Prue knew that pushing the tower of crates was her only means of escape.

But could she really risk injuring—or killing—her sister?

It's not Phoebe anymore, a voice screamed in her mind. Look at her. She's a zombie. Prue hesitated, looking from her sister's deadened face to the stack of crates.

At that moment Helene moved in. Prue felt the zombie's fist slam into her temple. Then everything went black.

Feeling uneasy, Piper checked the glowing neon blue clock above the bar.

More than ten minutes had passed since Prue left for the ladies' room. She should have been back by now.

What if she'd already slipped out and somehow missed Piper? In this madhouse it was entirely possible. And if Prue was wandering around the club looking for her, Piper would be better off staying right here near the door to the restrooms, where she had told Prue she would be.

On the other hand, what if Prue had gotten into trouble in the ladies' room? This did look like a pretty rough crowd.

Making up her mind, Piper set her still-full beer bottle on a nearby table and opened the door marked Rest Rooms. She found herself in a long hallway.

As she made her way past groups of other people, she thought of asking them if they had seen Prue. But they all seemed to be in a world of their own, giddy partiers in masks and beads who had no idea that serious trouble might be lurking in their midst.

Piper hurried to the door marked Ladies and pushed it open. Inside she found a line of women waiting to use a handful of stalls.

"Hey, can't you see there's a line?"

"Wait your turn!"

Piper ignored the angry shouts and hurried to the row of stalls. She bent over to check the shoes beneath the doors. Prue had been wearing white canvas tennis shoes. The feet she saw were clad in stiletto heels, espadrilles, and pink leather flats.

"What are you doing? Get in line," said a gruff voice behind her.

Piper turned to see two huge, tattooed women glaring at her.

She had no idea which of them had snarled at her, but it was clear that they were both prepared to do battle over the bathroom stalls if it came down to that.

"Oh, I don't have to . . ." Piper cleared her throat.

They took a menacing step toward her.

"Look, I was just looking for my sister," she quickly. "She came in here. You haven't seen her, have you?"

She described Prue, turning so that she was talking not just to the two tattooed women, but to everyone waiting in line.

It was a waste of time, she realized. Nobody

was even listening, and there was no sign of Prue anywhere.

Her heart racing, she left the ladies' room. About to turn and make her way back to the bar, she noticed a door marked Exit.

She hesitated only a moment before pushing it open.

She peered out into a deserted alleyway. Her eyes scanned the parked cars, the Dumpster, the stack of packing crates.

Prue wouldn't have come out here without me, Piper told herself. Prue was too levelheaded, too responsible to have done anything but gone to the bathroom and come right back to where Piper had said they'd meet.

So then, where was she?

Piper closed the door and retreated back down the hallway to the club. "And then there was one," she murmured. A chill raced down her back as the phrase left her lips.

She spent the next hour roaming through the club, her eyes peeled for Prue. She looked for Andre behind the bar, thinking she could ask him if he'd seen her sister—either of her sisters, actually. But she didn't see him anywhere either.

Feeling frighteningly abandoned, Piper finally left the club. There was nothing to do but go back to Gabrielle's.

And what if nobody is there? asked a voice in her head. Where will you go then?

Somebody grabbed her from behind and spun her around.

Piper shrieked, clawing blindly at the strong arms that held her.

"What's the matter, baby? Don't you like to dance?" a voice slurred.

Laughter erupted around her. She opened her eyes to see a splotchy, unfamiliar face leering at her. Just some messy drunk and his crowd of drunken friends, she realized. She pulled herself out of his grasp in disgust.

The drunks staggered into the next raucous bar. Piper kept walking. She became conscious of the parade of bizarre passersby, of the carnival-like atmosphere that seemed more grotesquely distorted the farther she went. People seemed to leer from the windows she passed, smirking at her.

More than once she thought she spotted Prue or Phoebe in the crowd. Each time her heart raced and she did a double take, only to find bitter disappointment upon seeing a stranger's face.

By the time she turned down Gabrielle's quiet side street, tears trickled down Piper's cheeks. Had her sisters met some terrible fate, and was she powerless to save them?

She had almost reached Gabrielle's door when she felt a hand on her shoulder.

She spun around, half expecting to find that she'd been accosted by another drunk. But when she saw a familiar face, her breath caught in her throat. She gasped. "Randy!"

The Montagues' handyman stood behind her.

Piper's pulse began to race. What was *he* doing here?

She didn't know whether to be glad to see a familiar face or terrified. Reptile boy could easily be a part of that strange cult in the bayou.

"Piper, I'm glad I found you. Your sister's in trouble—"

"Phoebe?"

"She and Prue—both."

"How can you possibly know that?" Piper asked, narrowing her gaze at him. The only way he *could* know, she reasoned, was if he had been following her or if he had had something to do with what had happened to Prue and Phoebe.

"You have to trust me," he said hurriedly. "I'm here to help."

"Why should I believe you?" she asked. "Have you been following us?"

"Yes," he admitted. "But I swear, it's for your own good. I'm trying to help you, Piper. You've got to believe me."

"Then tell me the truth," Piper said. "Are you in league with Yvonne?"

"Yes," Randy answered.

Piper turned to run into the house.

Randy reached out a brawny arm and pulled her back to him. His face remained calm despite Piper's wild flailing against him. "Piper," he said, "there's a lot I haven't told you, and I'm sorry.

But we don't have much time right now. We've got to get back to the bayou."

"Why?" she demanded, her voice shrill with fear. "So you can feed me to the Petro loa?" She was shaking, unsure of whether Randy was about to save her life or end it.

"No," he told her. "It's true, I am a practitioner of voodoo. But I pray to the Rada loa." He released her arm. "Gabrielle and Andre are the ones who've got your sisters and Helene. They are the reason three lives are in danger."

Piper stared at him in disbelief. "That doesn't make sense. Why would Gabrielle hurt her own sister?"

"Because she lies with every breath she takes," he answered angrily. "And because she has made an angajan with a Petro loa who demands human sacrifices." He softened. "Piper, please. I know you have powers of your own. I need you to join them with mine if we're going to save your sisters. We have to work together."

He opened the door to his truck, which was parked on the sidewalk next to them. Piper wavered, unsure and frightened.

"Piper, *please*," he repeated. To her surprise she saw that Randy's jaw was trembling, almost as if he were on the verge of crying. "I was too late to save my own sister," he told her. "Let me help yours."

In the darkness Prue slowly became aware of a harsh pain in her skull.

Opening her eyes, she saw a blinding light and closed them quickly again. She was lying on her stomach, her cheek pressed against something cold and clammy. She inhaled and smelled the familiar scent of mud and algae. She heard crickets and night birds calling and realized instantly where she was—in the bayou.

Her mind drifted fuzzily, trying to comprehend how she'd come to be here. She dimly recalled being in the club with Piper. Then she had stumbled out into the alleyway and was attacked by Helene . . . and Phoebe!

Forcing her eyes open again, she glared into the light. It was coming from a fire that burned a few yards away. She turned her head slightly and saw that she was inside some sort of structure. Beneath her, the marshy ground oozed with swamp water, soaking her clothes. Yet, above her head was a thatched roof, held up by poles at the corners and in the center, not far from the fire.

An hounfort, she realized. This was a voodoo temple, the same one she'd seen with her sisters when they went searching for Helene.

A whip hung from the center post. The post was painted in bright bands of color. At its base was a wide circle of cement. Prue could see that it was stained with streaks of what looked like rust . . . or was it blood? That concrete circle was an altar, Prue knew. Offerings were made there. Perhaps even human offerings.

Prue became aware of movement around her.

She turned her head to see what it was, wincing against the crushing pain in her skull. She wasn't tied up, she realized. But that was because she was in too much pain to move. Helene had bashed her head, she realized. That must be why it hurt so horribly—and why she had blacked out.

Her view was blocked by a heap of sticks. She focused on them, trying to move them with her powers.

Nothing happened.

She tried again.

Still nothing.

Her powers had been incapacitated.

A chill went through her as she realized why. In the club—her beer must have been drugged. It was the only logical explanation.

Flinching in agony, Prue squirmed, inching her body along the ground until the sticks were no longer obscuring her vision. She strained to focus on the figures who had moved into her line of vision a short distance away.

With a sickening lurch in her stomach, she recognized Helene and Phoebe. Their eyes were vacant, as before; their movements robotic as they cleared a spot of ground under the hounfort.

Then two others came into view, their backs to Prue. Both wore hooded red robes and masks. One of them, the taller of the two, carried a long stick. With it, the figure began to inscribe something on the cleared spot of ground. Following his strokes, Prue recognized that it was a vèvè, the symbol of a Petro loa.

She recalled the one she had seen on the mirror in Helene's apartment—the interlocking triangles and swirls encased in a circle. Gabrielle had said it symbolized Zdenek, the loa of human sacrifice. Was this the same symbol? She had to know.

Prue strained to see, but again her view was blocked. This time, by the other, more slightly built figure.

There was something familiar about the way the slighter figure moved.

It's a woman, Prue realized, staring. She tried to focus her thoughts, but her head was throbbing. It was almost impossible to think clearly.

The hooded figure . . . who was she?

Prue searched the images that flitted through her memory.

"Yvonne," she uttered aloud, the obvious answer snapping into her mind. "Why are you doing this to me and my sisters?"

The figure froze, then turned. She reached her hand up to remove the mask from her face

"Gabrielle?" Prue gasped. Dazed, bewildered, Prue shook her head to clear it. The movement sent shards of pain to her very core.

The taller figure turned, his mask now discarded as well. From beneath the hooded cloak, Prue made out Andre's familiar dark eyes.

Prue stared as Gabrielle's lovely features twisted into a gruesome mask of hate. "*You* were

the one," Prue whispered. Suddenly she under-
stood everything. "You were the one with the
angajan, the one who made the deal with the Petro
loa. Not your sister. You lied about Helene . . .
about everything."

Gabrielle nodded, looking faintly amused.
"And you believed it so readily. You honestly
thought I was trying to help Helene, when really
she was trying to 'help' me. She wanted me out
of the secret société. And she was getting too
close—close enough to expose us. That's why I
was rushing home from San Francisco. Because
Andre told me Helene was going to find out all
about us."

Prue saw the look that passed between
Gabrielle and Andre. She realized in an instant
what was going on. "So you two are—"

"We work well as a couple, don't you think?"
Gabrielle asked with a laugh. "Remember that
conversation you overheard in the museum
about my poor sister? It was all for your benefit,
cher. And you believed every word."

Prue still couldn't quite take it in. "But you
and Andre?"

"You didn't really think he preferred that little
goody-goody to me, did you?" Gabrielle asked,
pointing toward Helene.

"But you're sisters, Gabrielle. How could you
hurt her? How could you turn her into a zombie?"

Gabrielle shrugged. "I had to stop her. But
then you got in the way at the airport."

"But . . ." Prue began again.

"Quiet!" Gabrielle yelled. With the toe of her shoe she kicked Prue in the stomach. Another stab of pain surged through Prue's body.

Prue coughed, struggling to regain her breath. Her gaze fell on the vèvè Andre had drawn. She frowned, studying it. Gabrielle continued to talk. Her tone took on an eerily conversational quality.

"Zdenek needs human blood to keep him happy. When you and your sisters were unlucky enough to anger me that day at the airport, I realized that the three of you would be the perfect sacrifice to keep Zdenek well fed and loyal. After all, I owe him. I called on him a while back to get rid of another obstacle standing between Andre and me."

"What obstacle?"

"Her name was Caroline something or other," Gabrielle said with a shrug.

Prue shuddered. Could Gabrielle really kill so casually?

"So now, thanks to Zdenek, and the Montagues, of course, it's just me and Andre," Gabrielle was saying.

Prue frowned darkly, looking into the blue eyes that had deceived her so thoroughly. "What about the Montagues?" she asked.

"Kane and Daphne?" Gabrielle smiled. "I knew they would keep you safe for me until I needed you. I pay them a hefty sum to keep close tabs on all my sacrifices. And it was so easy for them to slip Phoebe the poison."

"They poisoned Phoebe?" Prue gasped, remembering her sister's sickened state. "When? How?"

"Little by little. In her food. In her drinks. Too bad they wore out their usefulness. I had to get rid of them as well."

Horrified, Prue tried to absorb it all. Kane and Daphne were involved in the secret société, too. Not to mention Yvonne and probably Randy.

"I figured I would take Phoebe first," Gabrielle continued. "She was the youngest one—the weakest one, just like Helene. Then I would work on you and Piper." Gabrielle smiled wickedly. "But you were so tenacious—searching for your sister, meddling in my affairs. Now it's going to cost you."

Prue turned away in disgust. Had she and her sisters been surrounded by evil on all sides but been too oblivious to notice it?

"See that?" Gabrielle gestured at the concrete circle. "That's Zdenek's plate. You're going to make an excellent appetizer for him, Prue. Then Phoebe and Helene will provide the main course."

She paused, her gaze falling on something behind Prue. Her lips curved into a slow smile. "Oh, look. Here comes dessert."

Prue felt her heart thudding with dread. She knew that could only mean one thing—Piper. Piper had come to save her. And now she was about to fall into Gabrielle's clutches, too.

CHAPTER 11

Piper slid a sidelong glance at Randy. He nodded reassuringly at her.

Piper crouched down at the edge of the clearing and turned her gaze back to the strange structure a short distance away. The voodoo temple seemed different than it had the night Phoebe disappeared. The structure itself seemed to be vibrating with energy—negative energy. The temple was more alive somehow and far more dangerous than it had been before.

Piper made out the figures of Phoebe and Helene standing at the edge of the structure. Both of them were poised in such a stiff, wooden way that it was clear they were zombies. To the left, Piper could see Gabrielle standing over Prue's crumpled form on the ground. She thought she'd seen Prue moving, but she couldn't be sure.

Please let her be alive, she begged.

Gabrielle approached a man's form. "Andre," Randy informed Piper in a whisper. Piper nodded as Gabrielle and Andre talked, their heads bent close together. At last, proof that Randy had been telling the truth—at least, about Gabrielle and Andre being in league with each other.

Piper still wasn't sure that Randy only wanted to help her and her sisters. For all Piper knew, he could be working with Gabrielle and Andre. Instead of rescuing Prue and Phoebe, he could be delivering Piper to her death alongside them.

Or he could be a good witch, a follower of the Rada loa, as he claimed, and really here to help her sisters. Either way, Piper knew she had to do something to save Prue and Phoebe. If her plan went sour, she'd just have to come up with a plan B—fast.

Piper saw Gabrielle take something from the folds of her robe. It glinted in the firelight. Piper swallowed hard as she realized what it was—an enormous dagger.

"It's time, Piper!" Randy hissed. "Now!"

Piper leapt from the shadows and raised her arms, freezing time just as Gabrielle and Andre turned toward her.

In the hounfort, everything went still and silent.

"Randy?" she asked, turning to look at him.

"Hurry!" he said, grabbing her arm.

Piper stared. Randy *hadn't* been affected by the time freeze. That meant he must have been telling the truth about being a good witch. She let out her breath in a whoosh. "Thank goodness, Randy," Piper said as they broke into a run.

"Piper!" Prue cried, her voice weak.

"I'm coming, Prue!" she called back. Then Piper stopped short.

Another figure had emerged from the trees. Someone who, like Randy, had been unaffected by the time freeze: Yvonne.

"What are you two doing here?" Prue asked Randy and Yvonne, venom dripping from every syllable. "Didn't want to miss the dinner party I suppose."

"We're here to help," Randy said as he hurried over to Prue. "I've already explained it to Piper. Yvonne and I have been working together."

"On what, destroying us?" Prue spat the words as Randy stooped to help her to her feet.

"No, Prue. That's not it at all," Piper began. She threw her arms around her sister, folding her into a grateful hug.

"My sister, Caroline, disappeared almost a year ago," Randy explained.

"Caroline?" Prue echoed, frowning.

Randy nodded. "She'd been dating Andre. I suspected he was involved in a secret société. But Caroline was young and headstrong and not about to listen to her older brother." His voice dropped. "Her body was never found. But I know Andre and Gabrielle did something to her here in the bayou."

"Caroline," Prue said, nodding. "Gabrielle just told me about her. She and Andre *were* responsible for what happened to her, Randy. They considered her an obstacle. I'm so sorry."

"Me, too," Piper said, squeezing his hand. The touch sent goose bumps up her arm. Then she realized—the time freeze. She had no way of knowing how long it would last. "What do we do about Phoebe?" she asked. "And Helene?"

Randy turned. "That's where Yvonne comes in. She is a Cajun healer," he said. "Her powers are pretty amazing."

"I have been attempting to keep you safe. You and your sisters," Yvonne explained. "I took Phoebe's hair to use in a protection spell. I put the vèvè in her room to ward off evil. But I underestimated Gabrielle. The magic I used to combat her was not powerful enough." She paused. "Now I know what I am dealing with. Now I am ready to fight."

Prue, clinging to Piper's hand, asked in a choked voice, "Do you think you can heal Phoebe?"

"Perhaps, cher, though I have never tried to restore life to a zombie." The old woman walked slowly past the fire, its flames frozen in place. She passed the motionless figures of Gabrielle and Andre.

Piper and Prue exchanged a glance. Piper knew that her sister was thinking the same thing she was. At any moment the time freeze could wear off.

Work fast, Yvonne, Piper prayed silently.

They watched as Yvonne circled Phoebe.

Once.

Twice.

As she circled a third time she raised her hands and began to chant in her thick patois.

Piper watched in amazement as Yvonne reached into her pocket and drew out a small sack. As the woman raised it in the firelight, Piper whispered to Randy, "What is that?"

"Salt," he said quietly. "It's a powerful purifier. Yvonne is using it to purify the poisons from their bodies."

Yvonne poured a small pile of white crystals into her hand. Then she held her palm close to Phoebe's face and blew the salt toward her. Then she began to chant again and to use the salt to trace symbols in the marshy ground.

Slowly Phoebe's eyelids began to flutter.

Piper gasped as Phoebe blinked, then looked right at her and Prue, a confused expression on her face.

"Phoebe!" Piper shrieked.

She and Prue broke into a run, embracing Phoebe so hard they nearly knocked her over.

Yvonne had blown the salt onto Helene, and now she, too, was returning to life.

"What . . . what's going on?" she asked, sounding dazed.

"Oh, Yvonne, how can we ever repay you?" Piper exclaimed. She turned toward the old woman.

Yvonne was stooped over, and suddenly Piper realized how fragile she was, despite her magical powers.

Randy rushed forward and put an arm around Yvonne's shoulder. "That took everything out of her. We've got to get out of here before Piper's spell wears off." He was already ushering Yvonne and Helene away from the hounfort.

Piper grabbed Phoebe's arm and then Prue's to lead them away. Both her sisters swayed unsteadily, still shaking off the effects of what they'd been through. "Hurry!" Piper urged them.

Just as they slipped through the trees, Piper felt the time freeze ending. She could hear Gabrielle and Andre shouting at each other, furious at having lost their captives.

Yvonne steadied herself against the trunk of an oak tree. "We must stop them," she said. She reached into her pocket, fumbled around for a moment, then handed Prue what looked like a yellowed sheet of parchment.

"What is that?" Piper asked, looking over her sister's shoulder.

"The words written here are an ancient spell," Yvonne said. "You must utter the name of the loa at the end."

"And this can stop Gabrielle and Andre?" Piper asked.

"This will do far more than that. The spell will banish the Petro loa, himself. But it requires tremendous power." Yvonne sighed. "I'm not strong enough now. Not after the healing. But with the three of you . . . perhaps you can banish Zdenek once and for all."

"Without the evil loa, Gabrielle and Andre can't harm us—or anyone," Helene added.

"She's right," Randy agreed. "Are you willing to give it a try?"

The Charmed Ones nodded.

"All right then," he said.

"Shh . . . listen!" Yvonne cautioned.

Piper heard chanting.

She turned and saw Gabrielle and Andre standing by the fire in the hounfort, their arms raised, their heads thrown back.

She didn't understand most of the words that escaped their throats in the weird, high-pitched incantation. All at once an icy breeze stirred the trees overhead.

The gust grew steadily stronger, howling around them. Piper shivered against the sudden chill in the air. The sky had grown black, the moon suddenly obscured by a roiling mass of clouds.

"Look!" Phoebe said, pointing.

Piper saw a thick, enormous black snake rear up beside the flickering fire, looming high above Gabrielle and Andre.

"What kind of snake is that?" Piper asked.

"It . . . it looks like that thing from my vision," Phoebe told her. "The one where the snake was going to devour that girl."

"That's no snake. It's a loa," Randy muttered as the monstrous creature turned its head toward them. Its eyes were twin pinpoints of flame. Deadly fangs jutted from its mouth. Piper had never seen anything that was so purely evil.

"It's seen us!" Yvonne exclaimed. "This is it. You must use your power now if we are to escape."

Stepping out of the shadows, the three Halliwell sisters joined hands. They advanced slowly on the hounfort.

"The Power of Three," Piper called out to steel her sisters. They squeezed her hands.

"The Power of Three," they answered back.

Piper saw Gabrielle's face smirking beside the serpent, heard Andre's voice booming as he continued the chant.

Prue held the yellowed paper up in front of them. She began the incantation, her voice sure and strong. Piper chimed in, along with Phoebe.

Piper focused every shred of her being on the lethal reptile that towered above them, its tongue darting out at them from between strong jaws.

They reached the end of the chant, and Piper felt herself shuddering with terror. The humongous snake hadn't disappeared. If anything, it just looked angrier.

The spell hadn't worked!

"Oh, that was very impressive," Gabrielle said, laughing. "Don't you know you can never win against the power of the loa? It's too strong for you."

"You should have remembered that yourself, Gabrielle," Randy said, stepping forward from the shadows. He held up a charm—a silvery object that shone in the firelight.

Piper recognized the series of interlocking triangles and swirling lines surrounded by a circle. It was a vèvè—the one that belonged to Zdenek.

With a flourish Randy threw it into the circle.

Instantly there was a rushing sound in the sky overhead.

Piper looked up. A shriek she hardly recognized as her own filled her ears.

Above her an enormous vulture circled. Its eyes glowed an unearthly fire red.

Stunned, Piper realized that Randy's spell hadn't worked either. Instead, he had called another deadly loa to the scene. Terror filled Piper's mind. They were all going to die.

CHAPTER
12

Prue heard a bloodcurdling scream as the massive black vulture swooped low.

She braced herself, feeling the rush of wind as the vast, beating wings brushed just overhead. She could feel her sisters cowering on either side of her. She clung tightly to Piper and Phoebe's hands as she waited for the inevitable.

But the unearthly monster swooped past her, past all of them.

In utter shock she realized that the vulture had landed outside the hounfort, a few feet away from the hissing snake.

"What did you do?" Piper screeched at Randy. "Now there are two of them. We'll never be able to hold them both off."

"We won't have to. Watch," Randy told her.

"Noooo!" Gabrielle howled. She fell to her knees, her arms outstretched. "The loas," she sobbed wildly. She clutched Andre, and the two cowered against each other, as though they could make themselves invisible to the two monsters. "They've seen each other," she cried. "We're doomed!"

The black vulture opened its sharp, curved beak and screamed at the snake.

The snake hissed wildly, black venom dripping from its open jaws.

"What are they doing?" Phoebe whispered to Prue, her gaze fixed on the enormous creatures.

"It looks like they're going to attack each other," Prue answered, mesmerized.

But the reptile turned away. Now it slithered toward Gabrielle and Andre.

"No, Zdenek, please! I beg you!" Andre screamed.

The serpent ignored his pleas. It began to coil itself around Andre's robed legs, its thick body winding higher and tighter until only Andre's head could still be seen.

As Prue watched in astonishment, the snake, with Andre in its grasp, vanished.

Then the vulture took flight, swooping low over a terrified Gabrielle. It closed its immense beak around her waist and lifted her into the air, disappearing into the night in a rush of beating wings and swirling mist.

The fire that had burned in the center of the

hounfort began to spread. Huge flames devoured the wooden poles and licked at the thatched roof. In a matter of seconds, the entire structure was ablaze.

Prue turned to Yvonne, who stood beside her now. The old woman caught her eye and nodded slowly. "It's over, cher," she announced.

"But what happened?" Piper asked.

"The vulture was the Petro loa Zdenek, wasn't it?" Prue asked Yvonne. "Randy conjured it with the vèvè."

Yvonne nodded. "But what about the snake?" Phoebe asked. "I thought that was the Petro loa."

"It was a Petro loa," Yvonne told them. "The one Gabrielle and Andre conjured when they drew its vèvè on the floor of the hounfort."

"But that vèvè was different from Zdenek's!" Prue exclaimed. "Gabrielle and Andre weren't summoning Zdenek. They were summoning another loa."

"Prue is right," Yvonne said. "Gabrielle violated one of the strictest codes of the secret sociétés. One can worship and serve one loa, but not two different loas."

"And it cost her her life." Helene spoke for the first time. "Andre's, too."

"Oh, Helene . . ." Piper and Prue embraced the girl, feeling the hot, wet tears that spilled down Helene's cheeks against their own skin.

Then Prue realized that her own eyes were tearing, too—for the sister that Helene had lost and for the sister that she herself had almost lost.

Prue turned to Phoebe, who stood with Piper's protective arm around her. Her head rested on Piper's shoulder.

"I love you," Prue mouthed over Helene's head.

Phoebe nodded and smiled.

Aloud, she said, "I love you too, Prue."

"You guys, I absolutely cannot believe I'm really here!" Piper chirped over the pleasant din of clinking silverware and upbeat conversation.

Prue smiled at her sister, watching her gaze around the elegant, candlelit restaurant in utter bliss. Remy's was like Piper's own personal Disneyland, Prue realized. She scratched absently at a bug bite on her cheek, courtesy of lying face-down on the marshy ground.

Piper turned to Yvonne, who sat beside her at the large round table. "I still can't believe you know Remy. I mean, I've read that he was inspired by the Cajun cooks he met in Louisiana's back country, but to think that you were one of them—wow!"

"I've known Remy since he was this high," the old woman said, holding her hand at a level below the table's surface.

"Thanks so much for getting us a table, Yvonne," Piper told her.

"No two-hour wait, either. Which is a good

thing, because I'm starving," Phoebe said cheerfully. Prue was happy to see that the rosy color had returned to her sister's cheeks. She seemed more lively than ever in the three days since their encounter at the hounfort.

"So am I." Prue smiled.

She gazed around at the other diners and the waiters hurrying past them with loaded trays. Turtle soup, étouffée, blackened catfish, jambalaya, fried okra. She wanted to try it all, being in the mood to celebrate at last. They had even managed to squeeze in some sight-seeing yesterday, after long, long naps. One of Randy's friends worked at a big chain hotel in New Orleans, and he had wrangled them a room after a last-minute cancellation. Prue had never in her life been so glad to see an ordinary hotel room. Sure, the place lacked the local color of Montague House. Then again, it didn't come with voodoo-freak hosts, either.

"I'm hungry, too," Piper was saying, "but I guess we should wait to order."

Prue followed her gaze to the two empty chairs across from her.

"Do you think they'll show up?" Phoebe asked.

"If anyone can talk Helene into coming, cher, it's Randy," Yvonne said. "I sent him over to her place this afternoon with some of my herbal tea leaves. One cup will lift her spirits."

Prue noticed a mysterious half-smile on her wrinkled face. "Are you up to something, Yvonne?"

"Nothing but good," the old lady said slyly. "Look, there they are now."

Prue turned to see Helene and Randy making their way through the crowded restaurant. His strong arm hung around her slender frame, as though shielding her. She seemed to be leaning into him, a trusting expression on her face.

"Yvonne, by any chance did that tea of yours contain some verbena root?" Piper asked.

"Perhaps, cher." The old woman chuckled. "Perhaps."

"Verbena root?" Prue looked puzzled. "What's that?"

"Oh, just a little something that's used in love spells," Piper told her quietly. "I guess our little competition over Randy is kaput," she told Phoebe. They all rose to greet Helene and Randy with warm hugs. Phoebe and Piper laughed at the joke and cheerfully welcomed Helene and Randy to the table.

"We're so glad you're here," Phoebe told Helene. "I know these past few days have been difficult for you."

Prue gazed at the lovely young woman sympathetically. She'd been shocked when Prue, Piper, and Phoebe filled her in on the whole truth about Gabrielle and her plans.

Helene nodded as she took her seat, a shadow crossing her lovely brown eyes. She looked down at the tablecloth for a moment. But when she glanced up again, she was smiling. "I certainly wouldn't miss your last night here."

"And you'll have to come to visit us in San Francisco," Prue said. She paused. She didn't really want to dredge up a painful subject, but she couldn't resist a question for Randy. "What happened to the Montagues?" she asked. "Were you able to find them?"

Randy frowned. "Kane and Daphne have vanished. No one's heard from them."

"And no one will, either," Yvonne said confidently. "It was time the evil in that house came to an end. Now it will rot in the swamp, as it deserves to."

Helene smiled. "Yvonne's right," she said. "The whole nightmare is finally over."

"And now for the beginning of our meal," Prue said, glad to change the subject. "I think our waiter has finally arrived." A dark-haired man had appeared at their table, dressed in pristine white clothing.

Piper's jaw dropped open as she gaped up at him.

"Yvonne, it's good to see you again, cher," he said, kissing the old woman on both cheeks.

"Remy, I'd like you to meet some friends of mine," Yvonne said, a twinkle in her eyes. She made introductions around the table.

Piper sat there speechless, unable to move.

"I hear you've been wanting to meet me," he told her.

She cleared her throat and found her voice at last. "Desperately."

"And how have you enjoyed your stay in Louisiana, ladies? Never a dull moment here, eh?"

Prue, Piper, and Phoebe looked at each other.

"Never a dull moment," Prue echoed, shaking her head with a grin. "*Definitely* never a dull moment."

About the Author

WENDY CORSI STAUB was born and raised in western New York State. She moved to Manhattan after college to become a book editor and sold her first novel five years later. She has written more than three dozen books for teenagers and adults, including suspense, historical and contemporary romance, mystery, biography, and TV tie-ins, and has ghost-written novels for celebrities. She lives with her husband and two young sons in suburban New York City.

YOU COULD WIN A DIAMOND HEART PENDANT JUST LIKE PRUE'S!

Cast Your Own Spell—Enter Now!
4 Chances to Win!

1 Grand Prize:
A diamond heart pendant just like the one
Prue wears on the show.
50 First Prizes:
A Charmed baby-doll T-shirt.

Enter now!
50 winners who enter from KISS OF DARKNESS will receive
a Charmed baby-doll T-shirt. More chances to win
in these upcoming Charmed books:

THE CRIMSON SPELL (April 2000)
WHISPERS FROM THE PAST (June 2000)
VOODOO MOON (August 2000)

Grand prize winner will be chosen from all entries received from sweepstakes in KISS OF DARKNESS,
THE CRIMSON SPELL, WHISPERS FROM THE PAST, and VOODOO MOON combined.
No purchase necessary. See details on back.

Complete entry form and send to:
Pocket Books/ "Charmed Sweepstakes"
1230 Avenue of the Americas, 13th Floor, NY, NY 10020

NAME_____ BIRTHDATE ____/____/____

ADDRESS_____

CITY_____ STATE_____ ZIP _____

PHONE_____

PARENT OR LEGAL GUARDIAN'S SIGNATURE (REQUIRED FOR ENTRANTS UNDER 18 YEARS OF AGE AT TIME OF ENTRY)

_____

See back for official rules.   **Book Code #C5**

2388-03 (1 of 3)

Pocket Books/ "Charmed Sweepstakes"
Sponsors Official Rules:

1. No Purchase Necessary.

2. Enter by mailing this completed Official Entry Form (no copies allowed) or by mailing a 3" x 5" card with your name and address, daytime telephone number, birthdate and parent or legal guardian signature if entrant is under 18 at date of entry to the Pocket Books/ "Charmed Sweepstakes", 1230 Avenue of the Americas, 13th Floor, NY, NY 10020. Entry forms are available in the back of Charmed books KISS OF DARKNESS (2/00) Book Code #C2, THE CRIMSON SPELL (4/00) Book Code #C3, WHISPERS FROM THE PAST (6/00) Book Code #C4 and VOODOO MOON (8/00) Book Code #C5, on in-store book displays and on the web site SimonSays.com. Sweepstakes begins 2/1/00. Please indicate the applicable book code # (i.e. C2, C3, C4 or C5) on your entry form and the envelope. Entries must be postmarked by 8/31/00 and received by 9/15/00. Not responsible for lost, late, damaged, postage-due, stolen, illegible, mutilated, incomplete, or misdirected or not delivered entries or mail or for typographical errors in the entry form or rules or for telecommunication system or computer software or hardware errors or data loss. Entries are void if they are in whole or in part illegible, incomplete or damaged. Enter as often as you wish, but each entry must be mailed separately. Grand prize winner will be selected at random from all eligible entries received. There will be 4 separate drawings for first prize winners and for each such drawing 50 winners will be chosen from all eligible entries received for each of books 2-5 in the Charmed series. Thus there will be 1 drawing for the entries received for KISS OF DARKNESS and 1 drawing for THE CRIMSON SPELL, etc. The drawing for grand prize and first prizes will be held on or about 9/25/00. Winners will be notified by mail. The grand prize winner will be notified by phone as well.

3. Prizes: One Grand Prize: A diamond heart pendant like Prue's (approx. retail value: $500.00). 200 First Prizes: A Charmed baby doll T-shirt (approx. retail value: $8.00 each).

4. The sweepstakes is open to legal residents of the U.S. (excluding Puerto Rico) and Canada (excluding Quebec) ages 12-21 as of 8/31/00, except as set forth below. Proof of age is required to claim prize. Prizes will be awarded to the winner's parent or legal guardian if winner is under 18 years of age. Void wherever prohibited or restricted by law. All federal, state and local laws apply. Simon & Schuster, Inc., Parachute Publishing, Spelling Television Inc. and their respective officers, directors, shareholders, employees, suppliers, parent companies, subsidiaries, affiliates, agencies, sponsors, participating retailers, and persons connected with the use, marketing or conduct of this sweepstakes are not eligible. Family members living in the same household as any of the individuals referred to in the preceding sentence are not eligible.

Charmed™

---

5. One prize per person or household. Prizes are not transferable and may not be substituted except by sponsors, in the event of prize unavailability, in which case a prize of equal or greater value will be awarded. All prizes will be awarded. The odds of winning a prize depend upon the number of eligible entries received.

6. If a winner is a Canadian resident, then he/she must correctly answer a skill-based question administered by mail.

7. All expenses on receipt and use of prize including federal, state and local taxes are the sole responsibility of the winners. Grand prize winner may be required to execute and return an Affidavit of Eligibility and Publicity Release and all other legal documents which the sweepstakes sponsor may require (including a W-9 tax form) within 15 days of attempted notification or an alternate winner will be selected.

8. Winners or winners' parents or legal guardians on winners' behalf agree to allow use of their names, photographs, likenesses, and entries for any advertising, promotion and publicity purposes without further compensation to or permission from the entrants, except where prohibited by law.

9. Winners or winners' parents or legal guardians, as applicable, agree that Simon & Schuster, Inc., Parachute Publishing and Spelling Television, Inc. and their respective officers, directors, shareholders, employees, suppliers, parent companies, subsidiaries, affiliates, agencies, sponsors, participating retailers, and persons connected with the use, marketing or conduct of this sweepstakes, shall have no responsibility or liability for injuries, losses or damages of any kind in connection with the collection, acceptance or use of the prizes awarded herein, or from participation in this promotion.

10. By participating in this sweepstakes, entrants agree to be bound by these rules and the decisions of the judges and sweepstakes sponsors, which are final in all matters relating to the sweepstakes. Failure to comply with the Official Rules may result in a disqualification of your entry and prohibition of any further participation in this sweepstakes.

11. The first names of the winners will be posted at SimonSays.com (available after 9/31/00) or the names of the winners may be obtained by sending a stamped, self-addressed envelope to Prize Winners, Pocket Books "Charmed Sweepstakes," 1230 Avenue of the Americas, 13th Floor, NY, NY 10020.